MARINE D: SBS

WINDSWEPT

MARINE D: SBS

WINDSWEPT

Peter Cave

First published in Great Britain 1995
22 Books, Invicta House, Sir Thomas Longley Road,
Rochester, Kent

A CIP catalogue record for this book is available from the
British Library

ISBN 1 898125 40 6

10 9 8 7 6 5 4 3 2 1

Typeset by Hewer Text Composition Services, Edinburgh
Printed in Great Britain by Cox and Wyman Limited, Reading

1

Samos, Greece, June 1984

'Bit bloody different to South Georgia, ain't it?' said Colin Graham, swigging his ice-cold bottle of Fix beer as he relaxed in the warm Greek sunshine.

'Too damn right,' Bill 'Sooty' Sweep readily agreed. The mere mention of the Falklands sparked off his all too recent memories, triggering an involuntary shiver as he remembered the biting cold and wind-driven rain of the bleak islands that he and his fellow British servicemen had nicknamed the 'Costa Hypothermia'.

Now, almost two years later to the day, the two Marines sat at one of the tables of a harbourside taverna on the island of Samos, enjoying the dry heat of early summer. But it was not a holiday. It was just another island, another year – and another mission.

'So what do you reckon they've cooked up for us this time?' Graham murmured. 'You can bet your bloody life we ain't here just to guzzle beer and eye up the birds for a couple of months.'

Sooty, who had been doing exactly that, managed to tear his attention away from a particularly striking pair of Nordic blondes for just long enough to consider the matter. Theorizing about the exact nature and purpose of their current military mission had probably been a popular pastime of every professional soldier since the days of Alexander the Great. But to members of the élite Special Boat Squadron, such reflections invariably had a special edge, for few assignments were ever simple, and most turned out to be highly dangerous. Here, though, in the relaxed setting of a popular holiday paradise, it was not easy to imagine where that danger might lie.

Sooty chose not to try. He took another gulp of beer and shrugged philosophically. 'I guess we'll know soon enough,' he muttered, returning his eyes to the undulating and beautiful pear-shaped arses of the two departing blondes.

Graham let it pass, indulging his own thoughts and not sharing his colleague's enthusiasm. He was strictly a tit man, and anyway he preferred redheads. In the absence of any in the immediate vicinity, his memories drifted back to the location of his original observation.

The Falkland Islands, 14 June 1982. He was on his first ever mission with 41 Commando SBS, having completed his specialist training at Royal Marines, Poole, only three months previously. Even those gruelling months had hardly prepared the tough cockney for the bloody baptism of real war.

A 'special hazard operation', they had called it – something of a euphemism for what was virtually a suicide mission. Joining forces with troopers of 22 SAS, they had set out to divert Argentinian attention from an attack by 2 Para on Wireless Ridge. Just a handful of men in four Rigid Raider boats against an estimated enemy force of 11,000. Slipping under cover of night into Stanley Harbour, they had orders to lay down a blanket of fire which would help fool the Argies into believing that a full-scale offensive was taking place.

Miraculously, and against all odds, the crazy plan had succeeded, despite the unexpected discovery of the small raiding force by the crew of an enemy hospital ship. Forced to retreat under a withering hail of small-arms fire, the joint force was lucky enough to suffer only four non-lethal injuries, although all four of the Rigid Raiders were so badly damaged that they later had to be scrapped.

But the daring ruse had achieved its objective. By first light, the Argentinian garrison was confused and preparing to retreat, convinced that the night raiders had been merely the first wave of a concerted British attack. Only a few hours later, Lieutenant-Colonel Mike Rose bluffed the enemy commander-in-chief, General Menéndez, into an unconditional surrender of all Argentinian forces.

It was all a far cry from his situation now, Graham reflected, sharing Sooty Sweep's view that it was difficult to imagine any kind of danger in their present idyllic surroundings. It was his first visit to the Greek islands, and although he had been there only three days he was already captivated by the serene beauty of the landscape, bathed in that wondrous light which is peculiar to the Aegean.

For a first visit, Samos was a particularly fortunate destination – although he had been given no choice in the matter. Largest of the Dodecanese group, and closest to the Turkish mainland, Samos, the legendary island home of the goddess Hera, was an emerald mounted in a bed of sapphires. Among the most verdant of all the Greek islands, its rolling hills and mountains were covered in the rich foliage of countless pine and olive trees, vineyards and aromatic shrubs, all set against the incredibly translucent blue of the surrounding sea.

A place of peace, Graham mused idly. Apart from the voracious mosquitoes, and the bold feral cats which seemed to be everywhere, a place in which any form of attack or predation seemed almost unthinkable.

Yet back at base, a mere nine kilometres along the southern coast and within sight of Turkey, Lieutenant-Colonel Gerald Martin had already established a full-scale arsenal of weapons and what amounted to an operational fortress.

It had to be for something, Graham reflected. And if the SBS were involved, it was unlikely to be anything pleasant.

2

Khania Harbour, Crete

Banners and flags fluttered everywhere, every one of them appearing to bear out the simple message that they proclaimed: 'The Wind is Free!'

But while that might have been true of the wind, it most certainly was not echoed by the hectic commercial activity which had transformed the usually quiet harbourside, Mike Bright reflected cynically. As far as the eye could see, on land and in the water, everything was very much for sale – from simple balloons and colourful kites to racing dinghies and luxury six-berth sloops.

Not that he had any argument with that. He had a strong vested interest in the proceedings, and indeed had been a prime mover in the organization of the international event which had virtually taken over the island for the past two weeks. As one of Europe's leading designers of both mass-produced and custom-built surfboards and sailboards, he had been one of the first people to realize the commercial potential of a major festival which would celebrate and promote the remarkable 1980s boom in wind sports. Tie such an event in with an equally booming holiday destination for British and mainland European tourists, and you were guaranteed a winner, Bright and his colleagues had figured.

So the First International Wind Festival had been conceived. Set against the magnificent backdrop of the Greek islands and using Crete as its base, it was a three-week showcase for every conceivable kind of leisure and pleasure activity involving wind-power. Exhibitions, demonstrations and displays of such diverse sports as windsurfing, hang-gliding, stunt kiting and sky-surfing were combined with championship contests for both prestige and big money prizes.

The festival had proved a huge success, surpassing the wildest hopes of its organizers. It had attracted manufacturers and potential buyers from all over Europe and beyond, along with hundreds of serious enthusiasts and thousands of tourists who had come along just to enjoy the spectacle. Not surprisingly, the event had also attracted the beautiful people – the young jet set and their inevitable hangers-on. The rich and overprivileged mingled with the package-tour holidaymakers and the penniless designers and prospective manufacturers hoping to make that vital personal contact or land the one big order which would set them up for life.

Not so different from his own situation only a few years ago, Bright reminded himself wistfully, remembering the bad old days when he had nothing to his name except a lease on a small fibre-glass moulding shop in Perranporth, Cornwall. His own big break had come when a chance meeting at a windsurfing qualifying round championship in Bude had brought Randy Havilland into his life. At that time merely a hopeful for the British championship title, Randy had outlined his own vague design for a really fast 'sinker' board and rig which would leave current sailboards standing in anything over eight knots of wind.

The rest, as they say, had been history. Bright's expertise, funded by Randy's lavish personal allowance from his wealthy merchant banker father, had resulted in the development of the prototype for what would become the Bright Barracuda, now one of the best-selling mass-produced sailboarding rigs in Europe. The original innovative design had given Randy Havilland the edge he needed to win the British Championship within three months, and its successors had carried him to his current status as reigning European Champion.

The partnership had endured, even if more by reason of mutual advantage than any real friendship between the two young men. Mature beyond his thirty-two years, and basically serious-minded, Bright had never been able to bring himself to actually like Randy, who, five years his junior, was essentially just a spoilt, vain playboy. But he was realistic enough to recognize and appreciate the joint benefits that the relationship brought with it. Randy gained the advantage of a personal and highly talented sailboard designer and Bright enjoyed the reputation and commercial advantage of equipping a champion. It had paid handsome dividends. Besides franchising his designs out to other manufacturers, Bright could now sell his own custom-made boards for upwards of £1500, and there was no lack of customers. But it was a tough, highly competitive business. To stay on top, you had to stay in the public eye by coming up with new ideas and fresh designs as well as keep tabs on the opposition.

Either of these reasons would have been more than enough to justify Bright's presence at the International Wind Festival. But there was another: Mike Bright thrived on challenge as much as Randy Havilland lived for publicity and public adulation. The Crete festival had offered them both a chance to indulge these individual needs fully in the form of the ultimate contest.

The Greek Islands Sailboard Marathon had been intended as the final highlight of the three-week event and something which would launch the sport of windsurfing into a new and more serious era. Starting out from Crete, contestants would have to make the 100-mile hop to the island of Naxos in one go, then complete a roughly circular course via Mikonos, Andros, Skiros, Chios and Ikaria before returning to Crete. It was a deliberately tough and demanding course of roughly 400 miles which would test both contestants and their equipment to the very limits. A contest strictly for fanatics — or fools.

Randy had been the hot favourite to win and Mike had held every confidence in taking home the designer's trophy for the event. Neither man had expected any problems.

But there *was* a problem – and it was a big one. Just two hours out from his second island checkpoint, Randy Havilland and his rig had disappeared without trace.

3

'Mr Mallory?'

The polite enquiry jolted Jim Mallory back to earth. His mind had been up in the sky above his head, along with the three graceful Bennett Seagull hang-gliders wheeling effortlessly on the updrafts of wind coming in from the sea and rolling up over the coastline.

Mallory turned to face the man who had addressed him, appraising him briefly before giving a nod of confirmation.

'Yeah, I'm Jim Mallory. What can I do for you?'

The man did not answer immediately. Instead he raised his eyes to the three kites, which were already beginning to lose height in long, lazy spirals.

'Beautiful, aren't they?' he said. 'And so quiet, too.'

Mallory shrugged. 'Yeah, they're beautiful all right,' he agreed almost grudgingly. 'But that's part of their trouble. They're designed far too much to look pretty than for sheer performance.' He pointed up at the sky. 'You see that angle of descent? Far too steep. Improve that by only two or three degrees and you'll have increased your soaring time by fifteen, maybe twenty per cent.'

'A problem you've already cracked, I take it?' The question was more like a statement, and totally devoid of any sarcasm.

Mallory studied the stranger more closely, his curiosity aroused. That the man was English was clear from his clipped, precise tone, yet there was something oddly stiff about his bearing which went beyond Mallory's image of the average uptight Brit. A military man, whispered the small voice of intuition. With this sudden hunch came the faint sound of warning bells inside his head.

Mallory looked at the man guardedly. 'So what's your interest? You don't look like a flyer.'

The man smiled thinly, hunching his shoulders in a faint shrug. 'Well, not hang-gliders, anyway. But you're right, of course – I do have an interest. Particularly in you, Mr Mallory.'

It was all becoming far too mysterious for Mallory's liking. His guardedness hardened to open suspicion. 'You know *me*?' he asked, making it sound almost like a challenge.

The man shook his head. 'No, but I know about you, Mr Mallory. James Clinton Mallory. Born Aubery, California, 1952. Probably one of the world's most innovative designers of hang-gliders and microlight aircraft.'

The warning bells in Mallory's head were ringing ever louder now, but he was already hooked. 'Look – what the hell is this all about?' he demanded.

Abruptly, the man offered his hand. 'You can

call me Gerald Martin,' he said quietly. 'And for
the time being let's just say that I might have a
commission for you.'

Mallory shook the man's hand warily, his suspicions in no way allayed by the formality of the
introduction. Indeed, if anything, it caused further
misgivings. 'You can call me Gerald Martin,' the
man had said. It implied an alias, deepening the
mystery. But for now, it seemed the name would
have to do, for the man was obviously in no hurry
to give further details.

'But before we get down to specifics, I'd like
to talk about microlights in general,' Martin went
on. He gestured towards the three Seagulls, which
were all just coming in to land some three hundred
yards further up the beach. 'For instance, just how
much radical design change can those things take
before it affects their basic aerodynamics?'

It was essentially a very simple question, with
a simple answer. Mallory shrugged faintly. 'Not a
great deal,' he admitted. 'There's reasonable room
for modification, certainly – but the fundamental
design is more or less fixed.'

The American broke off, his mind wandering
back to the early seventies, when he had first
become hooked on the fledgling sport of hang-
gliding – jumping off the cliffs above Big Sur, or
hopping over the sands of Santa Monica beach.
The early craft had been crude, dangerous and
strictly limited to short and strictly downhill glides.
No more than oversized kites, many of the first
hang-gliders had been built from nothing more

substantial than bamboo poles and plastic sheeting. Things had changed a lot in the past twelve years or so, of course. The new generation of machines were more like proper aircraft, capable of soaring and aerobatic manoeuvres rather than merely gliding – but they were still essentially Rogallo deltas.

Mallory snapped back to the present. 'How much do you know about the history and background of these things?' he asked Martin.

The man hunched his shoulders. 'Let's just assume that I'm totally ignorant,' he suggested.

It was an open invitation to launch into a potted history. Mallory drew a deep breath. 'OK,' he muttered, then nodded down the beach to where the trio of Seagulls were now parked, nose down, in the sand. 'Those three machines there are all second-generation designs,' he started out. 'They're fairly high performance, curved-boom craft, owing virtually all their design characteristics to the original triangular or delta wind-sail concept. That principle traces back to Francis Rogallo, a design engineer with NASA during the sixties. He came up with the idea originally as a possible land re-entry device for returning space capsules, but it was considered far more risky than the conventional parachute and wet splashdown techniques and eventually dropped.'

'So are you saying that Rogallo's original design is inviolate?' Martin wanted to know, interrupting. 'That there's nowhere else to go?'

Mallory shook his head. 'Not at all. What I am saying is that we're more or less stuck with the basic principle until something fairly radical comes along. Put it this way, Mr Martin – the Montgolfier brothers could no more have started out by designing a Zeppelin than Wilbur Wright could have flown a Boeing 737. Leonardo da Vinci designed an aerodynamically sound helicopter, but he was centuries too early for a suitable power source to make it fly.'

'So it's a matter of time?' Martin prompted.

Mallory shrugged. 'That, and a sufficiently strong incentive for a designer to approach the problem from a different angle.'

'Cold cash, for instance?' Martin suggested.

Mallory's eyes narrowed. 'What exactly are you after, Mr Martin?'

Martin spread his hands in a gesture which suggested openness. 'Suppose I asked you to design and build such a radically different flying machine?' he said flatly. 'Would you be interested in the challenge for $100,000 – cash in hand and no questions asked?' Martin paused briefly, the ghost of a twinkle dancing in his grey eyes. 'A down payment of $10,000 now, and the balance to be deposited in an American small-town savings bank of your choice – safe from the prying eyes of the IRS.'

Mallory allowed himself a thin, somewhat rueful smile. The Brit had obviously done his homework thoroughly. He knew more about Jim Mallory than just his birthplace and designing skills. For the moment, however, he played down his initial enthusiasm, using Martin's ploy of talking hypothetically.

'Just supposing I *was* interested in this proposition? Just what sort of a flying machine are we talking about? And, for that matter, what's it for?'

Martin was suddenly evasive again. 'I'd rather not go into any specifics just now. The point is, are you interested?'

Mallory made an impulsive decision, driven by the sense of adventure as much as the lure of the money. It was a decision that Martin had never doubted for a second, having had his man pegged from the very start.

The deal was clinched with nothing more than a faint nod from Mallory.

Martin smiled fleetingly. 'Good,' he said briskly, before gesturing down the beach to where the three hang-glider pilots were de-rigging their craft and furling up the wings. 'This part of the beach is completely deserted at night. Be here at exactly ten o'clock tonight with enough luggage for two or three days. A boat will pick you up.'

On finishing his little speech, Martin turned away, as if to leave. Mallory gaped at him. 'And that's it?' he muttered.

Martin nodded curtly. 'That's it for now, Mr Mallory. I have some other people to see back in Khania.' He turned away again, pausing on an afterthought. 'Oh, I almost forgot – sorry.' He delved into the pocket of his linen jacket, pulled out a bulky brown envelope and handed it over. 'Ten thousand dollars down payment, as agreed. Do count it if you wish.'

Mallory did count it. He was still flipping through the sheaf of $100 bills as Gerald Martin walked off the beach and disappeared as inobtrusively as he had arrived.

Mike Bright came out of the coastguard office at Khania harbour with a curse on his lips. Half an hour of frenzied gabbling in his limited Greek and a great deal of pidgin English had got him exactly nowhere.

The laid-back attitude of the local people which made the islands such a relaxing holiday venue became like a brick wall when it came to trying to get anything actually done. As a result, Bright had been totally unable to instil any sense of urgency in the authorities about Randy Havilland's disappearance. Far from initiating any sort of search-and-rescue operation, they seemed to be unconvinced that there was any sort of problem, let alone danger. A series of careless shrugs and polite but meaningless smiles were the only response to his most urgent pleas.

Bright was left in no doubt that the authorities considered that any fool who ventured out into the open sea on nothing more than a contraption of fibre-glass, aluminium tubing and Dacron deserved everything he got. If any kind of a search was to be mounted, it was clearly up to Bright to organize it himself. With this thought heavy in his mind, he walked slowly round the harbour towards the nearest taverna, to sit down and think things out over a glass of ouzo.

'Ah, Mr Bright,' Gerald Martin said crisply, appearing from nowhere and falling into step beside him. 'Please don't worry yourself unduly about your friend. Mr Havilland is perfectly safe, I assure you.'

Bright stopped in his tracks. 'What the hell are you talking about?' he snapped. 'Who are you anyway?'

Saying nothing, Martin took his arm in a deceptively casual gesture, propelling him firmly towards the nearest table. He sat down, summoning the waiter with a click of his fingers. 'What will it be, Mr Bright?' he asked politely.

Bright sat down, glaring at him across the table. 'Ouzo,' he grunted. 'And a jug of iced water.' He waited until Martin had ordered himself a beer and dispatched the waiter before launching into the questions buzzing around in his head like summer flies.

'What do you know about Randy? And where the hell is he? What's going on around here?' he blurted out.

Martin smiled reassuringly. 'As I told you, he's perfectly safe – you have my word for it. In fact, I have a message from him for you. Mr Havilland requests that you join him. "Tell Mike to get his arse here double quick," I believe were his exact words.'

It sounded like Randy all right, Bright thought. He eyed Martin suspiciously. 'Where is he?' he repeated.

The waiter returned with the drinks and set

17

them down on the table. Martin took a sip of
his beer and wiped his lips before answering.

'He's on another island, with some colleagues
of mine. If you're prepared to cooperate with us,
I'll take you to him tonight.'

There was not the faintest trace of menace in
Martin's tone, but Bright's guts tightened. There
was only one possible conclusion, and he jumped
to it. His eyes narrowed to slits.

'What is this? Some sort of kidnap?'

For a second Martin looked genuinely shocked.
Then his face cracked into a grin. 'Good Lord,
no,' he protested. 'Is that what you thought? I'm
so sorry, Mr Bright – I must have given you a
completely false impression.'

Bright was even more bewildered, and a little
thrown. 'You haven't given me any sort of an
impression yet,' he complained with some feeling.
'All you've given me is bits of some crazy bloody
puzzle that doesn't make any kind of sense.'

Martin was apologetic, even if he wasn't yet
prepared to be perfectly candid. 'Look, all I can
repeat is that your friend is perfectly safe and well,'
he said in a calm, matter-of-fact tone. 'He is with
us by choice, of his own free will – although at the
specific request of his father, I do have to admit.
There is absolutely no question of any kind of
coercion, and certainly no attempt at extortion.'
Martin broke off to reach in his jacket pocket and
draw out a buff envelope. 'In fact, Mr Bright, I
have some money to give to you, if you'll be good
enough to join us.'

He dropped the envelope on the table. 'There's £5000 in there. A ten per cent advance of the £50,000 we are willing to pay you if you decide to help us in a little design project. It's right up your street, I assure you – and I honestly believe you'd enjoy the challenge.'

Still highly dubious, Bright picked up the envelope, tore it open and gently shook it to half expose the contents. He did not have to see the whole of the banknotes to realize they were genuine. He shook them back into the envelope, leaving it on the table to show Martin he was not playing ball.

A young woman was approaching their table. Martin stood up politely to greet her, pulling out a chair. 'Miss Reece, I'm so glad you decided to accept my invitation.' Martin glanced at Bright as Janice Reece sat herself down. 'I invited Miss Reece to join us. I believe you already know each other.'

Bright simply nodded, giving little away. There might be some sort of psychological advantage to be gained by concealing the true extent of his relationship with Janice Reece for the moment. Martin appeared to be the man with all the secrets, so perhaps one of his own might not be a bad idea.

Not that it was much of a secret, Bright had to admit to himself. Half a dozen casual dates which had suggested that there might be something more than just physical attraction, but nothing really conclusive. Their busy lifestyles had ruled out sustained contact, although they bumped into each other from time to time in a business capacity. As a leading designer of wetsuits and possibly one of the best sailmakers in the business, Janice tended to move in similar circles to himself.

Perhaps sensing Bright's reticence to greet her more openly, Janice was also cool. She smiled at him across the table. 'Hallo, Mike,' she said.

Martin seemed suddenly embarrassed, perhaps sensing that there was something more personal between the two young people. He pushed himself up from the table somewhat abruptly. 'Look, I have a couple of telephone calls to make,' he said quietly. 'I'll leave you two to have a little chat for a couple of minutes. Please order yourselves whatever drinks you would like.' He nodded down at the money in the envelope, still on the table. 'I'll leave that here, as a token of good intent,' he said to Bright. Delving into his pocket again, he produced yet another envelope, which he dropped down in front of Janice. 'And this is for you, Miss Reece.'

He walked away, leaving the couple in something of a vacuum. Neither spoke for several seconds.

Finally, Bright broke the silence. 'Have you got the faintest idea what's going on here?'

Janice shook her head, then picked up her envelope. 'Not a clue, Mike – except that he wants us to work on some kind of joint project, and there appears to be an almost unlimited amount of money available.'

Bright nodded at the envelope. 'What did he offer you, if you don't mind me asking?'

Janice shrugged. 'Ten thousand,' she said candidly. 'How about you?'

Bright grinned briefly. 'A little bit more,' he admitted. 'Who the hell is he, do you think?'

Another shrug. 'God only knows. But I'll take an evens bet that he's connected with the military in some way.'

'Woman's intuition?' Bright asked, smiling.

Janice shook her head. 'Woman's powers of observation. The way he moves, the way he holds himself – lots of things.'

Bright grinned. 'I'd never have taken you for a forces sweetheart.'

Janice let it go. 'Point is, what do we do about it?'

It was a good question. Stumped for a good answer, Bright could only speculate. 'Maybe I have less choice than you do. He says he's got Randy.'

Janice's eyes widened. 'You mean holding him hostage?'

It was Bright's turn to shrug hopelessly. 'That's what I thought. But apparently not. It seems to be a bit more complicated than that. He claims Randy is cooperating at the request of his old man.' Bright paused. 'Whatever's going on, it seems to have been thought out pretty carefully.'

'So are you planning to go along with it, then?' Janice wanted to know.

Bright smiled ruefully. 'The way I see it, there's not much else I can do. Randy might need my help, and I owe him at least that.' He looked at Janice quizzically. 'What about you?'

By way of an answer, she picked up the envelope on the table and slipped it into her handbag. 'Let's put it this way,' she muttered. 'I haven't had a better offer this week.'

Out of the corner of his eye, Bright could see Martin returning. He reached quickly across the table, took Janice's hand and gave it a quick and reassuring squeeze. 'Just watch your back, that's all,' he hissed quietly. 'At least until we have a better idea of what we're getting into.'

4

As Martin had promised, the beach was quiet and deserted. Mallory paid the Greek taxi driver, who gave him a brief, vaguely pitying look before stuffing the bundle of banknotes into his pocket and driving off into the night. It was not his function to question the strange ways of tourists, just to take their money. Why anyone should want to transport a large holdall to a small and deserted cove in the middle of the night was none of his business. Anyway they were all crazy – the English, the Germans, the Swedes and particularly the Americans. There was only one good thing about them, and that was they never argued about the fare.

Mallory watched the lights of the battered taxi disappearing back up the rough dirt road with a faint sense of finality. He was committed now, to whatever little adventure he had managed to get himself into. Short of trudging back the eight miles to Khania in the dark, he had no choice but to wait for the promised pick-up.

He stepped off the road and on to the beach itself, his boots crunching against the fine shingle. Pausing at the water's edge, he stared out across the black water, straining his eyes and ears. There was no sound, other than the faint lapping of the Aegean against the shoreline. A barely discernible crescent moon cast little light upon the surface of the sea and in the darkness the twinkling lights of Khania harbour were no more than a vague, flickering glow further up the coast. It was a night, and a place, staged for intrigue as surely as a Hollywood film set, Mallory reflected fancifully.

The faint sound of an approaching car engine came to his ears, and he whirled round to stare inland again. In the distance, a pair of dancing headlights announced another vehicle approaching the cove by the same dirt track the taxi had taken. It was too much of a coincidence to be unconnected. Mallory waited expectantly for the vehicle to draw nearer.

It was some sort of open, four-wheel-drive vehicle, possibly a jeep, Mallory realized as it finally pulled into the small lay-by overlooking the beach. Again, the vague suspicion that he had got himself involved in some kind of military operation stirred in the recesses of his brain. He waited on the beach as the jeep discharged four passengers and then drove off again.

Abruptly, the beam of a powerful torch snapped on, carving a path through the darkness towards him. Temporarily blinded by the unexpected glare, Mallory threw his hand up over his eyes as the party stepped down on to the beach and began scrunching their way towards him.

'Ah, Mr Mallory. You're here early, I see,' came

Martin's precise, clipped voice. 'Just as well. I'll let
our water taxi service know we're all assembled.'

Martin held up the torch, pointed it out to sea
and switched it off and on again five times. Finally,
he set it down on the beach, to beam out over the
dark water. Like a beacon, or a homing signal,
Mallory thought.

His eyes had adjusted to the dark again, but
he could now make out all four figures in the
overspill of the torchlight. He recognized Martin
immediately, and identified the rest of the party
as two more men and a young woman. Martin stepped forward, making the introductions as
casually as if they had all met for some impromptu
beach party.

'I suppose we'd all better get to know each
other,' he announced brightly. 'We are going to
be together for a while – not least of which will
be a twelve-hour boat trip to our destination.' He
touched Mallory lightly on the shoulder. 'Mr Jim
Mallory – a cousin from across the big pond,' he
said warmly. He nodded towards Bright and Janice.
'Mike Bright, Miss Janice Reece,' he announced,
before gesturing towards the fourth man. 'And this
is Sergei Pavlaski. You'll all have to forgive him if
he's not terribly chatty. Mr Pavlaski is a Russian,
and doesn't speak very much English.'

Mallory reacted to this last introduction somewhat aggressively. Like many Americans, he had a
deep-seated and instinctive distrust of the Russians.

'What the hell is a goddamn Russki doing on
this little picnic?' he demanded of Martin. 'And

why the hell the need for all this cloak-and-dagger stuff anyway?'

It was a question which Martin once again chose to evade, glancing at Mallory with a look of feigned surprise on his face. 'Cloak-and-dagger stuff, Mr Mallory? Aren't we being a bit melodramatic?'

Mallory might well have made an angry response, but he was cut short by the sound of two powerful outboard motors rapidly approaching the beach.

'Ah, our transport is here,' said Martin, sounding slightly relieved. He bent down to pick up the torch again, and waved it slowly from side to side. In the sweeping beam, a low, flat, open craft could be seen heading in towards the beach, its engines dying back as it neared the shoreline.

Mike Bright appraised the boat carefully, taking a few seconds to identify its type. 'Rigid Raider,' he muttered, more for himself than for general information.

But the identification had not gone unnoticed by Martin. 'You know your seacraft, Mr Mallory,' he observed in a tone which suggested faint irritation.

Bright nodded. 'Dell Quay Rigid Raider, modelled on the Dory 17 hull,' he went on. 'Length 5.2 metres, beam 2.2 metres, draught 0.25 metres. GRP construction, virtually unsinkable and capable of up to 35 knots when fitted with twin 140hp Johnson outboards.'

Despite his vague annoyance, Martin was impressed. 'Yes, you do indeed know your craft,' he said quietly. 'Correct in every detail, in fact.'

Bright had taken in more information. Closer

inspection of the craft had revealed that it was completely stripped out, with nothing more than a pair of rolled-out inflatable air-bags to provide the absolute basics of comfort for passengers. It was no pleasure craft, that was for sure.

He turned on Martin, his voice taking on a more suspicious edge. 'These little beauties aren't exactly common on the commercial scene,' he pointed out heavily. 'In fact, their most usual application is purely military.' Bright broke off to draw a breath and glare at Martin accusingly. 'Which puts this whole little ball game into the realms of the navy – or more specifically, the Royal Marines. Still correct in every detail, Mr Martin? Or should we start addressing you by your correct rank, whatever that is?'

Faced with a direct challenge, Martin could only sigh regretfully. He had little choice but to open up. 'You're a very observant man, Mr Bright,' he conceded. 'Yes, your assumption is correct. This project is under the auspices of the military, although your help is being sought in a purely civilian capacity. None of you will be involved any deeper than as advisers, should you choose to cooperate – which I sincerely hope you will, by the way.' Martin paused to flash Bright a rueful smile. 'And my rank, since you ask, is lieutenant-colonel. But a simple Mr Martin, or even Gerald, will perfectly suffice.' He nodded towards the waiting Raider. 'Well? May I at least still have a couple of days of your time? You will all be properly compensated, I assure you – whatever happens.'

There were several moments of silence as each member of the party reassessed his or her position in the light of Martin's revelations. For Mallory, it merely continued his suspicions, and if anything had even heightened his sense of curiosity. Bright was having serious misgivings, but felt a sense of entrapment. His own position was not quite as clear-cut as that of the others, who had only themselves to consider. He had also to think of Randy, and what his involvement entailed. On balance, it seemed premature to back out.

Janice's doubts were based purely on practical matters of comfort, and she voiced them. Nodding towards the Rigid Raider, she said to Martin: 'You mentioned a twelve-hour voyage. I hope you're not expecting us to make the trip in that?'

Martin shook his head, grinning faintly. 'My dear Miss Reece, I wouldn't dream of asking you to consider such deprivation. This craft is here merely to ferry us all to a large and extremely well-equipped six-berth motor cruiser moored in deeper water. The bulk of the voyage will be in great comfort, I assure you.'

Martin jumped aboard the Rigid Raider, and beckoned them to join him. 'Well, lady and gentlemen, shall we depart?'

The single objection, now answered, seemed to act as a catalyst for all of them. With no more than a brief, questioning glance at Mike Bright, who could only shrug back at her, Janice moved towards the open boat and stepped aboard. Bright and Mallory followed her, making themselves as comfortable as was possible on the inflatable cushions. Pavlaski boarded the craft last, having said nothing and appearing to accept his role meekly as something which was predestined. Both Mallory and Bright suspected that he knew as much about what was going on as Martin, but the language barrier would preclude him as a source of information.

With everyone more or less settled in, Martin nodded to the craft's pilot, who, throttling up the twin Johnsons, backed the Rigid Raider back off the shingle and swung round in a slow, lazy arc before heading out across the open sea. Ten minutes later they were all clambering up the boarding ladder of a magnificent sixty-foot motor cruiser anchored in deep water. Probably specially chartered for the occasion, Bright thought, noting that the Greek crew all appeared to be civilians.

The Raider and its pilot pulled away, presumably back to a base somewhere on Crete. Martin ushered his guests into the motor cruiser's lavishly equipped stateroom as the twin Mercedes inboards throbbed into life. They were underway, destination still unknown.

5

Martin looked at them all in turn with the genial beam of an indulgent host as the white-coated Greek steward served drinks. Bright noticed that he avoided alcohol himself, settling for a plain glass of iced Perrier water. An on-duty rule, Bright wondered, or a teetotaller? But there were no clues to be gleaned there. He turned his attention to his fellow guests instead.

'Jim Mallory,' he muttered, sidling up to the tall Californian. 'The microlight designer and pilot, right?'

Mallory nodded, smiling. 'You got it.' He accepted Bright's proffered hand and shook it warmly. 'You in the same business? I don't know too many of you Brit flyers.'

Bright shook his head. 'No, I like to stay firmly on the ground. Or on the water, actually,' he corrected himself hastily. 'I make sailboards.'

Mallory looked blank.

'You probably call them windsurfers,' Bright added, realizing that the American was probably not familiar with the term.

Finally Mallory nodded. 'Oh, right.' Then he was

again thoughtful for a while, before eyeing Bright curiously. 'So where's the connection, I wonder?'

'Connection?' It was Bright's turn to appear dim.

'Between your field and mine. Martin approached me with some half-baked idea about designing a new type of aircraft. So what could he possibly want with a windsurfer designer as well?'

Bright could only shrug and say: 'Bloody good question.'

Mallory nodded at Janice, who was attempting to make conversation with the Russian but having little success. 'And your chick? What does she do?'

'She's a sailmaker,' Bright volunteered. 'And she's not exactly my chick, as you put it. More of a friend – a good friend.'

Mallory nodded again, his eyes still on Janice. For a second, Bright was sure he noted a faint look of satisfaction cross the Californian's face, and for some reason felt a twinge of jealousy.

'So what have we got?' he said briskly, steering the conversation back on track. 'A microlight designer, a sailboard designer, a sailmaker, a mystery Russian – and a British naval officer. A curious little mixture, wouldn't you say? Give you any ideas?'

The American shook his head slowly. 'Nope. None that I can think of right now, anyways,' he admitted. 'What do you think?'

Bright sucked thoughtfully at his lower lip for a few seconds. 'I think it's about time we demanded some answers,' he said, glancing sideways towards Martin.

'Yeah, I'm with you on that,' Mallory said firmly. Together they moved towards the only man who held the clue to the mystery.

Martin was smiling as they approached, although his eyes held a guarded, almost apprehensive look. 'And what can I do for you two gentlemen?' he asked politely.

'Dammit, Martin,' Bright burst out. 'You know bloody well what you can do. You can start giving us some clear and unequivocal answers. Starting with exactly where we're going and why you've gathered us all together like this, and what exactly you want us to do.'

Martin allowed himself a thin smile. 'That's a lot of starters, Mr Bright,' he pointed out. 'What exactly did you have in mind for the main course – the meaning of life, perhaps?'

Mallory was unimpressed with the attempt at sarcasm, and put in his own two cents' worth. 'Cut the crap, Martin,' he snapped. 'Bright's right – it's about time you told us exactly what we're all doing here.'

Martin's reaction to the sudden outburst of anger was unexpected. Far from putting him on the defensive, it seemed to raise his own hackles. He glared at Bright and Mallory with a look which was almost contemptuous.

'Look, there's one thing I will tell you right now,' he said gravely. 'I'm no happier about this set-up than you are. Just for the record, I fought this thing all the way down the line, ever since it was first suggested that I and my men had to work with a bunch of bloody civilians.'

'Don't you mean amateurs?' Bright suggested, reading between the lines.

Martin let out a short, mirthless laugh. 'I suppose I do,' he conceded. 'The point is, I have to follow my orders, whether I like them or not, and I have to make the best of it. Now, all your questions will be answered in good time, and you'll each be given every opportunity to back out if you so choose. But for the moment I can only ask that you make the same concessions that I'm having to make.'

Martin stopped talking abruptly, leaving Bright and Mallory somewhat thrown off track. It was the first sign that Martin was anything but in full control of the situation, and it put things in a different perspective. Suddenly he was as much a victim of circumstances as they were, and it seemed to create some kind of a bond between them all. The two men lapsed into a stunned silence.

Martin eventually spoke again, addressing Bright. 'All I can tell you now is that each of you have been chosen for your particular talents. We will discuss how those talents are to be used at a later date. As to why you're here at all, perhaps your friend Randy Havilland will best be able to explain, because I'm not sure that I could.'

Martin paused again, eyeing both men expectantly. 'Well?'

Bright and Mallory exchanged a brief, questioning look and both shrugged.

'All right. No more questions for now,' said Bright.

Martin looked relieved. 'Good. Then I suggest we all have another couple of drinks and then berth down for the night. We'll be arriving at our destination around 10.00 hours tomorrow morning.'

Bright was up on deck, staring out over the prow rail as Janice stepped up to join him. She appraised the green, rolling hills above the small harbour they were rapidly approaching before glancing at her watch. It was exactly ten o'clock.

'Spot on time for arrival,' she observed. 'But where exactly are we?'

'Samos,' Bright muttered, answering her. 'That's Pythagoria harbour directly ahead of us.'

Janice was impressed. 'You can recognize it from here? All harbours look pretty much the same to me.'

Bright nodded. 'Actually I know the whole island quite well. I spent a couple of seasons out here instructing sailing courses back in the seventies.'

'Good memories?' Janice asked.

Bright grinned mischievously. 'I can't remember,' he admitted. 'I seem to recall being stoned out of my head most of the time. Samos was one of the main inflow routes for kif and hash smuggled across from Turkey. Probably still is.' He fell silent as a thought struck him, his face suddenly serious. 'Jesus Christ, I wonder if that's what all this is about?'

Janice looked baffled. 'Not sure I follow you.'

Bright shrugged. 'I'm not sure if I follow it myself,' he admitted. 'But it might just help to explain what the British military could be doing here.'

Janice's curious look was an open invitation to explain further. Bright voiced the vague theory taking shape in his head.

'Suppose the Greek authorities were having trouble controlling the drug smugglers,' he hypothesized. 'It might make sense for them to call in some outside help. The Greeks are also looking for closer ties to mainland Europe at the moment, with eyes to full EC membership – so why not approach Britain? And who better to help solve their little problem than the Royal Marines?'

'You have a very fertile imagination, Mr Bright,' came Martin's voice, suddenly, from behind them.

Bright whirled round in surprise, feeling an unwarranted sense of guilt, like a conspirator caught in the act. He had not been aware of Martin's approach. It was as if the man had the ability to materialize out of thin air.

Martin was smiling at him indulgently. 'As I said, a very fertile imagination. However, you do have certain of your facts right.'

Bright faced him with a level gaze. 'What facts, for instance?'

Martin shrugged. 'Most of them, actually. Yes, this is Samos; yes, it's still a popular landing point for drugs; and yes, the Greek authorities do have something of a problem controlling it. However, nothing whatsoever to do with us, I'm thankful to say.'

The motor cruiser's engines had dropped to idling speed as they approached the confines of the outer harbour.

'Anyway, I suggest you both start getting your things together,' Martin said. 'We'll be berthing in less than ten minutes.' He turned and walked away, disappearing down the nearest companionway.

'Well, so much for that little theory,' Janice murmured, with a wry grin.

But Bright was unconvinced. Martin had been too ready to concede certain points for his liking. Almost as if the man had been trying to play something down by considering, then rejecting, its possibility.

He shook his head doubtfully. 'I'm not so sure,' he said quietly.

The route taken from Pythagoria only served to heighten Bright's suspicions. Disembarking from the cruiser, Martin ushered them all towards a small minibus, which promptly headed up the steep hill from the harbour then followed the high coastal route around the south-east side of the island for about three miles. From the rough geography of the island in his memory, Bright assumed that they were headed for Samos Town, and was surprised when the bus finally turned off from the main highway again and began to descend back towards sea level down a rough and very rutted dirt track.

After a couple of miles the road degenerated into little more than a cart track. The bus crawled between wild, gnarled old olive trees, through patches of rough scrub and bumped over patches of loose rock and shale where the track and the vegetation, disappeared completely. They continued to lose height as they drew ever closer to the brilliant blue Straits of Samou. On the far side of the water, the coast of Turkey was now clearly visible as a flat, light-brown strip of land rising into ridges of low hills.

'Where the hell are we now?' Janice asked, leaning forward across Bright's chest to look out of the bus window. 'You recognize any of this?'

Bright cast a quick look over his shoulder. Martin was seated at the rear of the bus with the Russian, Pavlaski, four seats behind them. He nodded faintly, lowering his voice to a mere whisper.

'Last time I was here, this whole area was under the control of the Greek military,' he hissed. 'It was all fenced off, regularly patrolled by armed guards – and according to rumour, heavily mined.'

'Mined?' Fear flushed in Janice's eyes. Her voice rose to a strangled croak. 'What the hell for? Are you telling me we could be driving through a bloody minefield?'

Bright gave her a reassuring smile, anxious to quieten her down. 'Relax, they must have cleared it all by now,' he said softly. 'But at the time, the Greeks were still jumpy about the possibility of a Turkish invasion, in the aftermath of the Cyprus conflict.'

'But you reckon it's safe now?' said Janice, calmer now.

Bright nodded emphatically, even though he

retained a few faint misgivings. 'Got to be, hasn't it?' he murmured. 'Martin may be a secretive sort of bastard, but I'm pretty sure he knows what he's doing.' He paused and sighed. 'But I'm still bloody suspicious about all these tie-ups with the Greek military. It just seems too much to be pure coincidence.'

'You could have a point there,' Janice whispered. She pointed ahead out of the bus window to a section of high chain-link fencing which had just come into view. Although sagging in a few places, it still looked as though it was maintained carefully, and carried a number of large warning notices at various points along its length. They were in Greek, and therefore undecipherable, but the distinct impression was one of stern warning. The fact that the fencing was still intended to keep people out was quickly borne out as the bus approached a pair of metal gates and ground to a halt.

Martin rose from his seat, walked briskly down the bus and motioned for the driver to open the door. Stepping out, he marched up to the gates, produced a key from his pocket and unlocked the robust padlock which secured them. Dragging them open, he waved the bus through and locked the gates again before reboarding.

Inside the fence, the bus continued across open scrubland for another half mile or so and finally began to descend a rough, winding track through what appeared to be a long-abandoned olive grove. When the bus eventually emerged from the trees, there opened up a vista of a picturesque horseshoe-shaped sandy cove, completely secluded by the rocky cliffs which encircled it. On a flat stretch of land adjoining the beach, a cluster of white villas gleamed in the fierce midday sun.

Janice took in the stunning view through the bus window with a little gasp. 'It's beautiful,' she breathed.

Bright might have been equally impressed, but his mind was on other things as the bus finally pulled up and the driver switched off the engine. The beach villas were obviously a private development of some kind, but it appeared oddly unfinished, and their position within a fenced-off area seemed unusual. He lay in wait for Martin as the small party began to disembark from the bus.

'So what is this place?' he demanded. 'And while we're on the subject, why is this area still fenced off? I would have thought the Greek military would have pulled out of all these coastal areas by now.'

Martin gave one of his infuriatingly condescending smiles. 'You really are a quite remarkable fund of knowledge, aren't you?' he said. 'How did you know this used to be a military area?'

'I guessed,' Bright lied, not caring whether Martin believed him or not. It seemed a sensible precaution to keep the full extent of his knowledge of the island to himself for a while.

Martin's face gave away nothing. 'How very intuitive of you,' he said. 'Yes, the Greek army maintained a presence here for some years. We just happen to be leasing the land temporarily.'

'And the buildings?' Bright prompted, jerking his thumb at the villas. 'Don't try to tell me those are barracks.'

Martin shook his head. 'Actually, it was a private development started by an Englishman working with a Greek partner. He ran into legal difficulties and eventually finance problems.'

It sounded feasible enough, Bright thought. He'd heard enough similar stories about the incredibly complicated problems of foreign investment in Greek property for it to have the ring of truth.

'Anyway, I'm sure you'll find everything perfectly comfortable,' Martin went on. 'Strictly limited main services, of course – but we have an adequate supply of fresh spring water and a back-up generator to supply us with all the power we're likely to need.' He seemed anxious to terminate the conversation. 'Perhaps we can continue this discussion later, Mr Bright. Right now I expect you and the rest of our guests would like to be shown to their rooms.'

Bright shook his head emphatically. Right now he had another priority. 'The first thing I want to do is to speak to Randy,' he said.

Martin nodded understandingly. 'Yes, of course.' He gestured to the largest of the villas. 'I expect you'll find him in the common room,' he suggested. 'We'll all be meeting there later, just as soon as everyone gets settled in.'

'And then some explanations?' Bright asked.

'Indeed,' Martin said curtly, with a faint nod. He strode away to gather up the rest of the party and escort them towards the villa complex.

6

Randy Havilland was doing one of the things he enjoyed most – sharing the company of a beautiful woman. He jumped up from his seat beside her on a long, low couch as Bright walked into the room. Grinning broadly, he bounded across the floor to greet his colleague enthusiastically, slapping an arm around his shoulder.

'Mike, I'm glad you decided to come.'

Bright's face was grim. 'You didn't leave me much choice, did you?' he pointed out. 'I thought you might be in trouble.'

The younger man adopted a feigned look of shock. 'Trouble? Who, me?'

Bright found his irrepressible good humour wearisome – and more than a little irritating after all the secrecy and vaguely threatening events of the past eighteen hours. He detached himself from Randy's grip, and after retreating to a safe distance turned to confront him. 'What the hell is going on here?' he demanded, more aggressively than he had intended.

It failed to make any impression on Randy, who continued to grin like a mischievous overgrown schoolboy. 'Hell, we'll talk about that later. Right now, come and meet Selina. Isn't she gorgeous?'

He led the way across to the young girl on the couch, giving Bright no choice but to follow. To have remained aloof would have seemed churlish. Not coincidentally, it also happened to be about the best invitation he had received all day.

Selina, it was true, was gorgeous. She was probably around twenty-six, Bright figured, although her smouldering Mediterranean looks made her look younger. A pair of full, pouting red lips and two sultry brown eyes stood out strikingly in a golden-olive, high-cheekboned face which was a perfection of symmetry. All this was topped by a shining mane of jet-black hair cascading over a body which made statues of Aphrodite look bloated by comparison.

Bright strode over to the sofa, smiling warmly and holding out his hand. 'Hi, pleased to meet you.'

Selina rose slowly, with all the sensuous grace of a cat. She took Bright's hand in a warm, firm grip and shook it formally.

'Hello, Mr Bright. Randy has told me a lot about you.'

'Mike – please,' Bright insisted. The girl acknowledged the informality with a faint toss of her head.

'Mike,' she corrected. 'So you're the man who made Randy a champion?'

Bright shrugged off the compliment. 'He did that himself,' he muttered. 'I just supply the hardware.' He expected Selina to sit down again, but she carefully smoothed out her skirt as though preparing to leave. 'I expect you have a lot to discuss with your friend,' she murmured politely to Bright. 'I'll leave you alone together.' With nothing more than another warm smile, she left the room.

Randy stared after her with the adoring eyes of a Labrador puppy. He was obviously badly smitten, Bright thought. Not an unusual occurrence, since he tended to fall in and out of love almost as regularly as the cycles of the moon.

'Who is she?' Bright asked, as Selina closed the door behind her.

Randy grinned. 'You name it, she's it,' he said. 'Sort of a resident chalet maid, I suppose you'd say. She's just here to cater to our every need – cooking, cleaning, that sort of thing.' He paused, letting out a regretful sigh. 'Well, not every need, of course – but I'm working on that.'

Bright digested this information apparently stoically, although his brain had already registered the fact that the girl somehow didn't seem to fit the picture. She hardly seemed the chalet-maid type. It was a job usually reserved for fairly simple peasant types, or at least girls of fairly limited education. Yet Selina had spoken to him in flawless English, suggesting a high degree of both education and intelligence. Her very bearing, too, exuded a degree of sophistication which seemed out of keeping with such a lowly occupation.

But for now, it was just another tiny piece of the general puzzle. Bright pushed the girl out of his mind and turned his attention back to Randy.

'OK, so what have you managed to get us both into?' he demanded.

Randy looked defensive. 'Hey, look, Mike. This wasn't my idea. I was just trying to win a race, for Christ's sake. First thing I knew about it was when these guys intercepted me out at sea and cut me dead in the water. Next thing I know I'm being hauled into some kind of fast patrol boat and told there's an urgent message from my old man.'

'Which was?'

'Here, read it for yourself,' Randy replied, pulling a crumpled fax from the back pocket of his trousers.

Bright took the single sheet and smoothed it out. The message was fairly brief: 'Dear Randy, I would deem it a great personal favour if you would cooperate with Lieutenant-Colonel Martin and his men. My appreciation will be reflected in next month's allowance. Regards, JR.'

Bright handed the paper back. 'JR?' he queried.

Randy grinned sheepishly. 'Jason Richard. The old man likes to use the abbreviation.'

'And that's it?' Bright asked, a trifle indignantly. 'All this cloak-and-dagger stuff is on the strength of one brief note from your father?'

Randy looked a little embarrassed. 'Perhaps you don't appreciate the significance of that last line,' he pointed out. 'Dad can express his disapproval as well as his appreciation through my allowance.' He paused, looking more serious. 'Anyway, there's a bit more to it than that. They brought me ashore, took me into Samos to buy some clothes and then I phoned home for some further explanation. Basically, it seems the old man made some sort of promise to one of his cronies in the Foreign Office.'

So the mystery had already progressed from the British military to the British Government, Bright thought, his head reeling. He eyed Randy curiously. 'Listen, Randy, I know your old man is a powerful financier and all that. But I didn't realize his connections went that high.'

Randy shrugged awkwardly. 'Probably just one of his gin-and-tonic drinking buddies at White's,' he said. 'At a guess, I'd say someone in a position to get him a few brownie points towards the knighthood he wants so much. Sort of a "scratch my back and I'll scratch yours" deal, I guess.'

Bright wasn't up in the ways of the City's old boy network, but Randy's explanation sounded reasonable enough. Not that it took him anywhere nearer to understanding what was going on, he reflected. 'So what's the deal?' he asked hopefully.

Randy spread his hands, a blank look on his face. 'Now you know as much as I do,' he muttered apologetically. 'We're both just going to have to wait until Martin is ready to fill us in with the details.'

Disappointed, Bright realized that once again everything came right back to Gerald Martin. He remained the single key which could unlock the mystery box. Whether or not it would turn out to be a Pandora's box remained to be seen.

Frustration demanded action of some kind. 'Shit,

I'm going for a stroll along the beach,' Bright announced irritably. It was a statement and not an invitation. He needed to be alone for a while.

A sudden thought struck him. 'I take it we are free to come and go as we please? I mean, we're not prisoners here or anything?'

'Not prisoners, exactly,' replied Randy, 'although the goon squad don't seem too keen on people wandering around too much.'

'Goon squad?' Bright looked blank.

'The rest of Martin's men. Our own personal security patrol. I take it you haven't met them yet?'

Bright was silent for a few seconds, trying to take it in. 'Are you telling me that we're all here under armed guard?' he blurted out eventually.

Randy grinned. 'Hell, no, not really,' he said cheerily. 'Sure, they carry guns around – but I'm sure it's just for effect more than anything else. You know what these guys are like – all that macho stuff. Cagey, too – that's why Martin is so tight-lipped about everything.'

Suddenly, Bright had the distinct impression that Randy knew more than he was letting on. Perhaps it was a trick he had learned from his father. He stared him straight in the eye.

'What are you talking about – *these* guys?' he snapped. 'And what macho image?'

Randy's eyes widened in genuine surprise. 'You really don't know what these guys are, do you?'

Bright could only shake his head dumbly, waiting for further explanation.

'They're SBS – Special Boat Squadron,' Randy went on. 'Hell, Mike, I thought you'd figured that out by now.'

Bright was dumbstruck for several moments, finally letting out his breath in a long, deep sigh. 'No,' he said heavily. 'I hadn't.'

7

Bright got the chance to assess the full strength of Martin's force over lunch, served in one of the villas, which had had all its interior walls knocked out to form a mess hall.

He counted five Marines besides Martin himself. Although they were dressed in a variety of nondescript clothing, from casual fatigues to T-shirts and chinos, it was still possible to identify them as a military unit, a small but highly trained and disciplined fighting force. Assuming that the pilot of the Rigid Raider was one of the group, and that at least one other man had been placed on guard duty while the others ate, it brought the full complement to eight, Bright figured.

Perhaps deliberately, Martin had arranged things so that he himself sat at the far end of the long single table with Bright, Mallory, Randy and Janice all isolated at the other. He made no attempt to introduce his men, or indeed to start any sort of a conversation at all as Selina bustled about serving what turned out to be an excellent lunch, even if the gathering was not particularly animated. It did not escape Bright's attention that she conversed apparently quite freely with Pavlaski in his native language while serving him, further confirming his theory that she was an educated young lady. He wondered, idly, how many other languages she spoke fluently and what other secret talents she possessed.

The meal over, Martin stood up somewhat stiffly. 'Well, perhaps we can all adjourn to the common room for coffee,' he suggested.

It was the signal for the five Marines to melt away back into the secretive little world of their own, leaving their lieutenant-colonel with the civilians.

'I wanted this to be as informal as possible,' Martin started, once they were all assembled in the common room. 'So I thought this would be the best place to hold a preliminary discussion.'

'Don't you mean preliminary briefing?' Bright called out, in a distinctly challenging tone. 'That is the correct term for a military operation, is it not?'

A thin, grudging smile tugged at the corners of Martin's mouth. 'Yes, Mr Bright, that is indeed the correct term. He scanned the room, flashing everyone in turn a look of apology. 'Very well,' he said eventually, with a faint sigh. 'Your first question answered. Yes, this is a military operation – fully sanctioned by Her Majesty's Government, by the way – and all of you have been co-opted as civilian advisers.'

If Martin had thought that the frank admission would help to defuse Bright's sense of curiosity, he had underestimated the man. Bright had the bit between his teeth now, and he wasn't prepared to settle for anything except the whole truth.

'Kind of unusual for you guys, isn't it?' he said pointedly. 'The SBS using civilians?'

A faintly annoyed expression crossed Martin's face for a second. Then he managed to smile again. 'Forget what you've seen in the movies,' he said to Bright. 'We're not the guys who wear our underpants outside our trousers. We don't leap over tall buildings at a single bound. What we do do is to use the finest men, provide the best training and use the finest equipment available to get the job done, whatever it is. Sometimes that means picking the brains of the best specialists and experts that we can get hold of. Which is where you all come in. Our sources tell us that in your particular fields, you're the best there is.'

Bright was still sceptical. 'All very flattering,' he said. 'But what exactly are you asking us to get involved in?'

It was Mallory's turn to demand some answers. He glanced at Bright rather than Martin, a confused look on his face. 'What are you getting at?' he asked. 'And what's this SBS outfit, for a start?'

Bright shrugged. 'I guess you guys would call them Seals,' he ventured, thinking of the nearest American equivalent.

Mallory whistled through his teeth, a look approaching awe on his face. 'Wow, those bastards are dangerous,' he said. 'They play rough.'

There was a hint of triumph on Bright's face as

he faced Martin directly again. 'Exactly my point,' he said quietly. 'Well, Lieutenant-Colonel?'

Martin was silent for a long while, apparently thinking deeply. Then he drew a deep breath and studied them all with a somewhat resigned expression on his face. 'Look, I think you're all letting things get a little out of perspective here,' he pointed out. 'Let's just forget the adventure comics for a while and look at the simple realities, shall we?'

Bright and Mallory exchanged a brief glance of acquiescence. It seemed only fair to give Martin the chance to explain things fully at last. Janice, who up to that point had remained silent, spoke for them all.

'Well, I never got round to reading Boys' Own adventures,' she put in. 'So I for one am quite willing to listen to the lieutenant-colonel's little scenario.'

Martin shot her a grateful expression. 'At the risk of sounding sexist,' he said, 'let me make the point right now that neither I nor any government department would condone the presence of a woman if there was any question of risk or danger involved.'

Janice thought the remark *was* sexist, but she let it go, assuming that Martin was talking from a sense of chivalry more than anything else.

'Your purpose here is basically very simple,' Martin went on. 'Each of you has a particular and specific talent. What we are hoping is that those talents can be combined in a unique way to tackle a unique challenge. Quite simply, we have three days in which to discuss the feasibility of a rather unusual piece of equipment. And, if we decide that the idea is feasible, to come up with some preliminary designs.'

'And what would be the purpose of this piece of equipment?' Mallory asked. 'I don't know about the rest of you people, but there's no way I'm willing to work on anything that might have military applications.'

Martin regarded the young man with a slightly mocking expression on his face. 'A pacifist, Mr Mallory? And an American, no less. You surprise me. I always imagined you people were raised on aggression and violence.'

Mallory chose not to take the observation as an insult. He merely fixed Martin with a look of sullen defiance. 'Yeah, well maybe Vietnam changed a lot of people's outlook on things,' he replied.

It was a point which Martin took to heart. His expression softened. 'Yes, I understand. But I think I can put your mind at rest. What we have in mind would have absolutely no offensive capability – you have my full assurance of that.'

'But it *would* have military application?' Bright put in, wishing to clarify an issue which he felt Martin had sidestepped rather neatly.

Martin nodded faintly. 'It might or might not be used in some future military operation,' he conceded. 'But in a purely peaceful manner.'

Having raised the issue, Mallory was unconvinced. 'That's probably what they told Einstein,' he said with heavy sarcasm. 'Sorry, Martin, but you're gonna have to do better than that. I want to know exactly what this "special piece of equipment" is, what it's supposed to do, and how you plan to use it.'

'I'm sorry. I'm not at liberty to give you any specific details at this stage,' Martin told him. It was not an apology, merely a statement.

Mallory thought for a while. 'Then we seem to have come to an impasse,' he said finally. He rose to his feet, glancing down at Bright and Janice. 'I can't speak for you two, but this is as far as I go.'

Martin let him get as far as the door. 'Just one thing to keep in mind before you leave, Mr Mallory,' he called out. 'Hundreds, perhaps thousands of innocent people – mainly civilians – may die needlessly if you walk out of that door. I think you ought to know that.'

Mallory stopped dead in his tracks, staring at Martin with a look of contempt on his face. 'That's the shittiest form of blackmail I ever heard, man,' he spat out.

Martin shook his head. 'No, that's the reality of the situation. Your expertise is crucial to this project. Without it, we can go no further.'

The American didn't like being put on the defensive, and it showed on his face. 'There are plenty of other designers in the world,' he pointed out, rather resentfully.

'Indeed there are,' Martin conceded, with a grim nod. 'But they're not here, right now – and time is the one thing we don't have much of.'

His hand still on the door handle, Mallory glowered at the man. 'You're a bastard, Martin. You know that?'

Martin allowed himself a wry grin. 'So I've been told – frequently.' He eyed Mallory like a hawk as he stood poised in the doorway, frozen in indecision.

Much of the conversation had passed over Randy Havilland's head – partly because it was in his nature not to examine anything too closely and partly because it was beyond his powers of imagination to visualize his own role in whatever was going on. However, Mallory's imminent departure, and Martin's reaction, warned him that the little adventure was about to come to an abrupt end. It would not please his father – and past experience had taught him that Jason Havilland's displeasure was invariably very expensive. He entered the discussion for the first time.

'Look, why not at least give Lieutenant-Colonel Martin the chance to outline what he wants?' he pleaded with Mallory. 'What the hell have you got to lose?' He glanced at Bright and Janice for support, a mute appeal on his face.

There was a long and heavy silence in the room, during which all eyes were on Mallory. Eventually he caved in under the subtle pressure. Still glaring at Martin, he walked slowly back to his seat. 'OK – as long as we're still talking purely hypothetically, I'll listen,' he muttered.

Martin's relief was obvious. He paused for a while, marshalling his thoughts and reflecting on the severe limitations he was having to work under.

It was a delicate assignment, and one that he had been loath to accept in the first place, but he was stuck with it. His orders had been clear – everyone was supposed to remain on a strict 'need to know' basis, including his own men. What had not been so clear was for how long he was expected to keep a bunch of naturally inquisitive and concerned civilians in the dark. Nor indeed how he was supposed to achieve such an impossible task. He felt a sense of gratitude towards Mallory as the young American opened up the conversation again himself, relieving some of Martin's sense of impotence.

'If you really need me for this little project, then you're talking about some sort of flying machine . . . right?' Mallory challenged.

'Right.' Martin confirmed this assessment with a curt nod. 'But it's not quite as simple as that.'

'So where do the rest of us come in?' Bright asked. 'As far as I'm concerned, anything above sea level is strictly for the birds.'

They had already reached the next rung in the 'need to know' ladder, Martin realized. It was time to ease things forward as subtly as he could.

'For the moment, let's just imagine that we were talking about some sort of hybrid, and purely hypothetical, type of craft,' he said guardedly. 'For the purposes of discussion, let's further assume that it would be part microlight, part hang-glider, part windsurfer and part surfboard. At some point, however, it might have to serve all these functions, and perhaps even more.'

Mallory laughed openly. 'Why not an anti-gravity machine with a time-travel option thrown in? Or would you care for a gizmo with an interstellar capability? You're talking fantasy stuff, Martin. The sort of shit fifth-grade schoolkids doodle on the back of their exercise books.'

Martin remained cool in the face of Mallory's ridicule. 'Think about it,' he urged. 'Really think about it. Obviously it wouldn't have to perform all these functions simultaneously. But how about one thing at a time? Some way in which it could then be stripped down and modified to meet the next requirement? Some sort of modular design . . . a multi-purpose kit, if you like.'

Mallory fell silent. Bright glanced up at Martin, a thoughtful look on his face. 'So what you want basically is a flying surfboard?' he said.

Martin scratched his chin. 'That's probably a wild understatement, but, yes, you have the general idea.' He looked towards Mallory. 'Well? Are we still in the realms of fantasy?'

The American was not overenthusiastic, although his expression showed that he had at least started to consider the concept. 'Even if the idea was work-able, what possible use would it be?' he asked.

It was a thinly disguised probe for further infor-mation, and Martin evaded it. 'That's not your problem,' he said flatly.

'With respect, Martin, it most certainly is our problem,' Bright interjected suddenly. 'How can we even start to design the thing unless we have a pretty fair idea of what it's going to be called on to do? We'll need a full list of functions, the sequence of those functions, and at least a rough guide to performance specifications.'

'And that's only for starters,' Mallory added. 'There are a thousand and one other factors in a design project that you guys don't seem to have even considered.'

Martin felt an inner glow of satisfaction, which he fought to keep from showing on his face. It seemed that the project had passed its first major hurdle. He had their interest now, and they were all rising to the challenge just as he had hoped they would. It was now surely only a short step before that interest could be whipped up into full-blooded enthusiasm. Now was the time to let a couple more tantalizing little snippets of information out of the bag, he decided.

'Let's make the basic assumption that this craft starts out its life as a powered hang-glider. Its first task would be to fly out over the open sea, preferably no more than twenty or thirty feet above the water.'

'How far?' Mallory interrupted. 'I'd need to know what sort of distance it'd have to cover.'

Martin looked a little surprised. 'Surely that's simply a question of how much fuel it starts out with, isn't it? The actual range of this hypothetical craft is something I would rather not be specific about at this stage.'

Mallory shook his head slowly from side to side, like a schoolteacher admonishing a backward child. 'It's not quite as simple as that,' he pointed out. 'Fuel/weight/range ratios have to be carefully calibrated at the initial design stage.'

Martin considered this for a few seconds. 'Then let's leave the whole question until such time as we do move towards an actual design,' he suggested. 'Remember – for the present, we're merely discussing feasibility.'

Mallory shrugged, accepting the compromise. Despite himself, he was already starting to become fascinated by the idea, and wanted to hear more. 'OK, so what next?' he asked.

'Our craft would then be required to make a landing on open water,' Martin continued. 'At which stage the engine would be detached and jettisoned, and the basic frame materials and wings stripped down and reassembled into the mast, boom and rigging of a windsurfer. With all extraneous parts dumped in the sea, it should then be able to complete its journey under wind-power alone, as efficiently and as inconspicuously as possible.'

Martin fell silent, leaving a hush in the room which lasted for nearly a minute.

'You're not really asking us for a pure feasibility study, are you?' Bright said at last, making the question sound like an accusation. 'Someone has already thought this thing through, haven't they?'

If he'd been caught out, Martin didn't show it, merely giving Bright a curt nod. 'In theory, yes,' he admitted. 'Our boffins came up with some rough sketches, but we decided we needed the help of experienced and specialist designers such as yourselves. Help that we're prepared to pay for, as I've already told you.'

'So, are there any other little tricks expected of this Heath Robinson contraption?' Mallory put in.

'Just one,' Martin answered. 'At all stages of its life it would suit our purpose if this craft were as indetectable as possible by all forms of surveillance, including radar.' He paused, allowing himself a wry grin. 'Invisible would be nice.'

It was the first time Martin had shown any sign of a sense of humour, Bright thought. Assuming he was joking, of course.

'I'm going to have to think about this,' he said. 'We all are.'

'Naturally.' Martin began to rise to his feet. 'I'll leave you to talk it over amongst yourselves. Let's discuss it again tomorrow morning after breakfast, shall we?'

He moved towards the door, then paused. 'Oh, by the way. You're all free to move around the village as you like, but I would prefer it if no one ventured on to the beach after dark.'

'Prefer?' Janice queried.

'It could be dangerous,' Martin replied. 'My men will be on patrol, and they're fully armed. A case of mistaken identity could be nasty.'

It was the first clear admission from Martin that the project was being treated as a full-scale military operation, and it gave them all food for thought.

'Are we expecting visitors?' Randy asked, half jokingly.

'I sincerely hope not,' Martin said firmly – and there was not the faintest trace of humour in his tone. He walked out of the room, leaving a puzzled silence behind him.

8

Martin snapped back to full consciousness abruptly, torn out of a crazy dream in which he had been flying on giant wings made from eagle feathers directly into the face of the blazing sun.

Awake now, he was in darkness, but just able to make out the vague shape of 'Sooty' Sweep bending over his bunk. The Marine's face was grim, though he managed a thin, apologetic smile.

'Sorry to wake you up, boss – but we might have a spot of bother.'

Martin threw his legs over the side of the bunk and jumped quickly to his feet. Automatically, he reached for his clothes folded neatly over the back of his bedside chair then paused. 'Outside?' he asked.

Sooty nodded. Changing his mind, Martin crossed the room and opened the small wardrobe. He chose a pair of dark trousers and a black polo-neck sweater, and pulled them on over his pyjamas, completing the impromptu outfit with a black Balaclava. His 9mm Browning High Power handgun was under his pillow, as it always was. Not bothering with the shoulder holster and harness, Martin tucked the gun directly into the waistband of his trousers and scooped out half a dozen spare clips from his bedside locker, and stuffed them into his pockets.

Having slipped on a pair of sturdy shoes, he was ready. The whole operation had taken less than thirty seconds. He turned to face Sooty again. 'What's the problem?' he asked, moving towards the door.

Sooty was already ahead of him as he answered. 'Maybe nothing – but there's some offshore activity up at the far end of the cove which could be a bit sussy. I thought it best to wake you and let you know.'

Martin nodded reassuringly. 'Yes, you did the right thing.' Following Sooty, he stepped out of the villa into the night air and dropped his voice to a whisper. 'Who else is on beach patrol with you?'

'Just Williams and Graham,' Sooty whispered back. 'Want me to alert any of the others?'

Martin shook his head. 'No, let's keep this as discreet as we can for the moment,' he said, thinking of the civilians asleep in two of the other villas, just yards away. 'As you say, it might be nothing. Just a bunch of trippers picking a bad spot to come ashore for a beach party.' He glanced down at his luminous watch as he spoke. It was three-fifteen in the morning, he realized. A bit late for a barbecue, and too early for breakfast.

They had reached the beach. Martin took the lead, treading lightly across the shingle towards the dim shapes of Colin Graham and Gareth Williams, who stood on the shoreline, both looking out over the dark water through night-vision binoculars.

'Anything happening?' Martin said quietly, aware that sound carried a long way over open water, especially at night.

Williams lowered his binoculars, passed them over his head and handed them to his commanding officer. 'Take a look for yourself,' he said. 'It's about a forty-footer, around eighty metres offshore to the right of the point. Haven't heard another sound since she cut engines and Sooty went to fetch you.'

Martin raised the binoculars to his eyes, peering through a dark-greenish mist until he finally identified the boat, which came into view like a semi-luminous ghost ship. It was, as Williams had estimated, around the forty-foot mark – too large to be one of the local caiques still used by the Greek fishermen, and with a low, flat superstructure unlike any pleasure cruiser Martin had ever seen. It definitely looked like a working boat of some kind, he thought – although what its crew could possibly be doing at this time of night he had no idea. He wondered briefly if the craft might be trawling for squid and octopus – an activity which often took place at night. But octopus fishermen invariably used bright lights to attract the creatures, and the boat was showing no illumination at all, either above or below decks. Besides, his cursory examination through the night binoculars had shown no signs of nets of any kind. So it was a mystery, and Martin didn't like mysteries, not on his patch, and especially when his current mission was of such a highly sensitive nature.

Lowering the binoculars, he turned to Sooty. 'They're not tourists,' he said confidently. 'I'd stake my life on that.' He directed his attention to Williams. 'What first made you suspicious?'

Williams grinned. 'All Welshmen are suspicious, boss. It's one of our national traits.' He adopted a more serious expression. 'Actually it was the way she came in. Very slow, single diesel virtually no more than ticking over and very muted. It sounded like they've got a muffler over the engine housing, and that stinks for starters. Want a shrewd guess?'

'Yes indeed,' Martin said.

'Six to four it's a drug-smuggling run,' Williams volunteered. 'They're probably just waiting for the buyers to show up and then they'll ferry the stuff in by dinghy.'

It was an explanation which had already occurred to Martin. 'Shit!' he said under his breath. 'That's all we need. The bloody Greek military assured me that they had this part of the coast firmly under control now. That's the main reason I leased this place as a base.'

'Get it cheap, did you, boss?' asked Williams. 'You know what they say about accepting gifts from Greeks.'

The attempt at humour was not appreciated. 'Not funny, trooper,' Martin hissed. 'So what are you suggesting we do about it? Let them unload their consignment of naughties and be on their merry way?'

The Welshman shrugged. 'We could do worse, boss. It might save any fuss.' He nodded his head back towards the villas. 'Besides, we've got our guests to think of. I thought you didn't want them spooked.'

It was a reminder that Martin didn't need. 'I don't,' he said firmly.

'So why not let them dump the stuff and run?' Williams suggested again. 'It's no real skin off our nose if another few kilos of hash finds its way into Greece. Besides, they're unlikely to use the same drop-off point twice, so this will probably be the last we'll see of them.'

Graham had been listening to the dialogue while keeping the boat under surveillance through his binoculars. Now he joined the conversation.

'I've got some bad news for you both,' he said quietly. 'Something tells me this is a lot more than just a few kilos of wacky baccy. These bastards are toting SMGs.'

Martin snatched up the binoculars again, training them on the boat. Two or three shadowy figures could now be seen moving about on deck, and the short, stubby shapes hanging from their shoulders were unmistakable.

'Shit,' Martin groaned. 'This could be heavy stuff.' He whirled on Sooty. 'Go and raise the rest of the men, as discreetly as you can,' he hissed. 'And tell Willerbey and Crewes to get into full scuba gear, just in case.'

'And break out the MP5s, boss?' Sooty asked, referring to the Heckler & Koch sub-machine-guns favoured by the SBS.

'Damn right,' Martin answered with a nod, viewing the safety of his men as his first priority. 'But I want to avoid any shooting if at all possible.'

'Got you, boss.' As Sooty set off for the villas, Martin tapped Graham lightly on the shoulder. 'How many?' he hissed in the trooper's ear.

Graham spoke without lowering the binoculars. 'I've counted only three so far,' he whispered back. 'But there might be a couple more still below decks.'

Martin took a certain amount of comfort from this assessment. Three amateur gunmen were no match for half a dozen highly trained Marines – under any circumstances. And for the moment, Martin and his men held the ace card in the element of surprise. There remained only the question of extra, unexpected visitors to consider. If the men on the boat were smugglers, then others would be coming to take delivery of their haul. As he waited for the rest of his men to turn out, Martin applied his mind to this aspect of the problem.

Corporal Bryan Bailey was patrolling the outer perimeter fence, he knew. Martin had enough trust in the man's abilities to feel confident that nobody could sneak past him. So the cove was protected from that direction, at least. The only other access would be from over the headland on the far left-hand side. If reinforcements were coming in, it would be from that direction only.

Martin tapped Graham on the shoulder again. 'I'll take over surveillance, Colin,' he whispered. 'You and Gareth fall back over the headland to intercept anyone else coming in.'

'Treat them as hostiles, boss?' Williams asked.

Martin nodded grimly. 'If they're carrying weapons, neutralize them,' he confirmed. 'Only try to do it quietly.'

The two men nodded. Pausing only to unhook the night-vision binoculars from around his neck and hand them to Martin, Graham fell into place beside his companion and the pair of them crept off into the darkness.

Martin returned his attention to the boat, where activity up on the deck had assumed a more definite purpose. Three of the gunmen were bunched together at the stern of the vessel, apparently in the act of lowering something black and bulky into the water.

The faint crunch of footsteps on shingle alerted Martin to the return of Sooty, accompanied by Simon Willerbey and John Crewes clad in their black neoprene wetsuits and trooper Andy Donnelly bearing four MP5s, one of which he handed to Martin wordlessly. Sooty had brought a large and bulky bergen, which he dropped quietly on to the beach at Martin's feet. 'I brought a few extra goodies as well,' he whispered. 'Just in case.'

Martin returned his attention to the activity on board the mystery boat. The bulky object was now clearly a two-man inflatable boat, which was dropped over the side. A couple of the armed men clambered over the stern rail of the boat, lowering themselves down into the inflatable on ropes.

So, it would be only two men to face, Martin thought to himself with some satisfaction. It raised the chances of ending any possible confrontation without the need for gunfire. He turned to the two men in scuba gear.

'There's a couple of these jokers coming ashore in an inflatable. They're carrying SMGs, so we can only assume them to be hostiles. You know what has to be done.'

Willerbey and Crewes nodded silently, both tapping the handles of the wicked-looking commando knives sheathed in their weight belts with a meaningful gesture.

The unspoken message was clearly understood. Martin jerked his head towards the sea. 'Let them get well clear of the boat,' he hissed as a final order. 'Just in case you're bumped and someone left on the boat takes a pot-shot at you, we'll have a clearer line of fire over your heads to cover you.'

The two frogmen pulled their masks down over their faces, adjusted their regulators and padded silently down the beach towards the dark mirror of the sea. Seconds later they had slipped into the water and were swallowed up in its inky blackness.

Sooty bent down, rummaging in the bergen and finally pulling out a powerful torch. He handed it to Martin.

'Here, I thought we could use this to divert their attention when the lads are ready to attack,' he said.

'Just a couple of brief flashes should be enough to make them wonder what's going on. They'll be so busy watching the shore for another signal, they won't know what's hit them.'

Martin took the torch gratefully. It was good thinking on Sooty's part. Although he had every confidence in Willerbey and Crewes making a successful surprise attack, it didn't do any harm to give them an extra bit of edge. He glanced down at his watch, estimating the time it would take them to intercept the inflatable and mentally counting off the seconds.

Finally taking up the binoculars again, he trained them on the stern of the boat once again, then brought them down slowly in a direct line towards the shore. The inflatable was about thirty-five yards clear of the boat now, and nearly halfway towards the shore. Willerbey and Crewes should be closing in now, he thought – if they were not already in position. After counting a further ten seconds, Martin held the binoculars in one hand and raised the torch and pointed it out over the water.

He thumbed the button twice in rapid succession, sending two brief beams of light out towards the inflatable. The effect was immediate, he noticed with satisfaction. The two men stopped paddling abruptly, and Martin could clearly see the two white blurs of their faces as they turned and gazed towards the shore. Almost simultaneously, he saw two sudden disturbances on the calm surface of the sea, one on either side of the inflatable. A pair of black shapes rose above the darker mass of the water, throwing themselves up over the rounded rubber sides of the small craft.

The occupants of the inflatable never stood a chance. Both men died immediately and soundlessly as one strong arm wrapped around each face and pulled the head back and another black arm drew the razor-sharp blade of a gleaming knife across their throats. It was all over in a split second. Martin continued to monitor the scene as Willerbey and Crewes slashed the rubber sides of the inflatable and then silently slipped back into the sea, leaving no more than two small rings of disturbed water and a few air bubbles. Only the savage hiss of escaping air echoing across the sea towards the beach showed anything had happened.

The sound had obviously been picked up on the boat as well, for suddenly a bright searchlight snapped on from the upper deck, beaming out over the surface of the water. It played for a while on the crumpled shape of the destroyed inflatable and the two bodies floating in the water, then swept in towards the shore.

Both Martin and Sooty were suddenly illuminated in the full glare of the beam. Temporarily blinded, each man's reaction was identical and immediate. They dropped like stones on to their bellies, rolling apart several feet before assuming a prone position and bringing the MP5s up into a businesslike position. Exposed as they were, they were like ducks on a fairground rifle range.

Martin tensed himself for a raking burst of sub-machine-gun fire from the boat, but it never came.

Instead the searchlight died abruptly, plunging them into darkness again. Seconds later came the sound of a diesel engine coughing into life and being hastily revved up. By the time Martin had retrieved the night-sight binoculars and trained them out to sea again, the boat had already described an arc in the water and was heading straight out towards Turkey.

Sooty pushed himself to his feet, slipping the safety-catch of his weapon back into position. 'Looks like we got off lucky,' he observed. 'They obviously didn't have the stomach for a fight.'

Martin rolled over on to his back and sat up, wiping sand and grit from his mouth with the back of his hand. 'Maybe they weren't looking for one.'

He rose to his feet as Willerbey and Crewes surfaced in shallow water and walked up the beach, peeling off their masks.

'Well, what was in the inflatable?' Martin wanted to know.

Willerbey shook his head in puzzlement. 'Bugger all,' he said flatly. 'Not a bloody thing. Strange, eh?'

Martin nodded thoughtfully. 'Very strange,' he echoed. He turned to Crewes. 'What about the occupants? Did you get any impression of who they might be?'

Crewes shrugged uncertainly. 'Greeks? Turks? All these Mediterranean types look pretty much the same to me, boss,' he said, then looked at Martin with a querulous expression. 'So if they weren't smugglers, what the hell do you think they were doing?'

It was a question Martin couldn't answer. 'Christ knows,' he said wearily.

'Do you want us to retrieve the bodies, boss?' Willerbey asked. 'They might tell us something.'

Martin considered the suggestion for a few seconds before saying: 'Where do you reckon they'll end up if we leave them?'

'The way the current appears to be running, my guess is that they'll eventually wash up over on the Turkish coast,' Willerbey ventured. 'They won't be coming back here, that's for sure.'

Martin made his decision. 'Then we'll leave them,' he said testily. 'Let the Turks sort it out. Dammit, this has caused me enough problems already.'

Now that the immediate crisis had passed, he was starting to get angry. Angry with the Greek military authorities who had assured him that the area was secure, and angry because the integrity and delicacy of his mission might have been compromised. He would have strong words with Selina in the morning. Martin happened to be the only other person on the island of Samos who knew that the girl was in fact a liaison officer with Greek Military Intelligence. Her very presence had been a condition of allowing the operation to go ahead. But liaison was supposed to work two ways, Martin thought bitterly. They would be strong words indeed.

Sooty brought him back to the present problem. 'So what do you want us to do, boss? Maintain full security patrol for the rest of the night?'

Martin shook his head. 'I don't think anyone will be coming back,' he said decisively. 'But you and Donnelly stay on beach patrol and stay in radio contact with Williams and Graham up on the headland. Wake me up again if there are any further developments.' He turned to Willerbey and Crewes. 'You two might as well catch up on your kip.'

With one last look out over the dark surface of the sea, Martin turned away and began to walk back up the beach towards the villas. At least the incident seemed to have been handled without disturbing the civilians, he reminded himself, looking for something positive. They remained crucial to the entire bizarre operation, and the less they knew about what was going on behind the scenes, the better. This consideration had figured largely in his decision to let the two bodies float off to wherever they might eventually wash up. Having two corpses to dispose of could have proved an embarrassment, to say the least.

Willerbey fell into step beside him as he walked up the beach. He said nothing, but glancing sideways, Martin could see the troubled expression on his face.

'What's the problem, trooper?' Martin asked.

Willerbey sighed, looking miserable. 'I'm just wondering about those two guys,' he admitted. 'If they weren't smuggling drugs, then what the hell were they doing here?'

Martin stopped in his tracks. He waited for Crewes to catch up with them before he spoke again, addressing them both. 'Look, let's get one thing straight,' he said. 'Our visitors weren't up to anything harmless, that's for sure. Innocent people don't sneak ashore from boats at night carrying sub-machine-guns. I had to presume them hostile, and you carried out your orders. It's what we do – remember?'

'Sure, boss.' Willerbey nodded, although he still didn't appear totally convinced. 'I just can't help thinking that we might have just topped a couple of Greek coastguards or similar. Maybe they were just another couple of poor sods on a military training exercise, or something like that.'

Similar doubts had already occurred to Martin himself, causing him his own moments of anguished doubt. But, for the sake of his men, he wasn't going to let it show. He spoke with quiet authority. 'Even if such an unlikely situation were possible, then it's not your responsibility,' he assured the two Marines. 'If anyone is responsible at all, it's the Greek authorities for failing to ensure this base was kept clean. We had a clear agreement, and everything was spelled out in no uncertain terms.' Martin paused briefly. 'Personally, I very much doubt if they would have broken it, knowing we were here. We do have something of a reputation, after all.'

Taking some comfort from the assurance, Willerbey managed a thin and rueful grin. 'Yeah, the rest of the world thinks we're a bunch of evil murdering bastards who shoot first and ask questions afterwards,' he observed. 'One of the many reasons we don't bring the subject of our occupations up on a first date.'

It was an ideal opportunity to inject a bit of savage humour into a grim situation – something which was standard practice in SBS circles. Crewes seized upon it.

'You mean you get dates?' he asked, feigning jealousy. 'You jammy bastard.'

Despite his misgivings, Willerbey smiled. Martin felt a sense of relief. Even with his training and the responsibilities of command, he was still sensitive enough to feel for his men when they agonized over a kill which was dubious, or might have been avoided. He racked his brains for anything else which might help put their minds at ease.

'What guns were they carrying?' he asked, as a sudden thought struck him. 'Did you get a chance to notice?'

Willerbey thought for a moment. 'One was definitely toting a Steyr MP 69,' he reflected. 'I'm not sure about the other guy.'

Martin glanced at Crewes. 'Well?'

The man shrugged. 'I didn't really notice,' he admitted. 'But it could have been a Czech Skorpion machine-pistol.'

'Then it's pretty safe to assume that they weren't on any official business,' Martin said firmly. 'All Greek military personnel carry Uzis as standard.'

The further reassurance seemed to cheer Willerbey up even more, although the last niggling little doubts were certain to remain. But that went with the territory, Martin told himself. Friendly fire, he thought without bitterness. It happened. It was always a very real danger of the job itself.

The three men continued to walk back towards the villas in silence.

9

The rest of the night passed without further incident, only increasing Martin's sense of frustration as he tried, without success, to get back to sleep. He lay on his back, staring up at the ceiling and almost willing Sooty to come charging back with news that they had intercepted further interlopers within the perimeter fence area. Even further hassle might have been preferable to not knowing anything.

It was not to be. Finally, as the first rays of dawn light began streaming into his room, Martin rose, dressed and strolled down to the beach again. He stared intently along the shoreline, from one end of the cove to the other.

Willerbey had been right. There was no sign of the two bodies, or of the wrecked inflatable. Only the figures of Sooty and Andy Donnelly patrolling either end of the beach gave any indication that the incident had been real and not just a bad dream. Both men had their backs to him. Martin sighed faintly to himself, turned and walked back to the kitchen to make himself a cup of coffee and wait for Selina to wake up.

* * *

He did not have to wait long. The girl was up long before anyone else. She looked only mildly surprised to find Martin waiting for her as she walked into the kitchen.

Martin rose from his chair, crossed the room and closed the door firmly. He studied Selina with a steady, penetrating gaze. 'We had visitors last night,' he said flatly.

Cool as a cucumber, the girl merely raised one perfectly trimmed eyebrow a fraction of an inch. 'Visitors?'

Martin gave her a brief run-down on the incident. When he had finished, he eyed Selina expectantly. 'Well?'

The girl shrugged. 'Smugglers,' she said, a little too dismissively for Martin's liking.

'The inflatable was empty,' he pointed out. 'Smugglers don't usually waste time by taking little boat trips in the middle of the night.'

'Then perhaps they were landing to pick something up,' Selina suggested.

Martin shook his head. 'That doesn't wash, either. My men scoured the whole area for the rest of the night. Nobody showed up.'

Selina studied his face for a few seconds. 'It seems to me that you're making an accusation of some kind, Lieutenant-Colonel,' she observed. 'You think I know something about this? Or even that I might have had something to do with it?'

Martin felt a trifle embarrassed. He wasn't very good with women. 'I'm not suggesting that,' he muttered defensively. 'Merely pointing out that your people assured me that this section of the island was completely under control. Also that there would be absolutely no interference from any section of the Greek authorities.'

'Ah.' Selina nodded, finally understanding the gist of Martin's suspicions. 'You're thinking that this was some sort of covert operation under our control?'

It was out in the open. Faced with it, Martin could only nod faintly. 'The thought had occurred,' he admitted somewhat sheepishly.

There was the faintest flash of defiance in Selina's dark eyes. 'Contrary to some popular beliefs, the Greeks are an honourable people, Lieutenant-Colonel. They keep their word. If you were promised a policy of non-interference, then that is what you will have got.' Her expression softened slightly. 'Besides – what would be the point? My presence here leaves no possible reason for the authorities to wish to spy on you. Even more to the point, they are fully aware of the secret nature of your mission and your ability to defend it. We don't run suicide squads.'

It was a perfectly logical argument, and one which Martin found impossible to counter. 'Which leaves us with a mystery,' he said with a sigh.

'Or perhaps no mystery at all,' Selina put in. 'Some potential drug smugglers simply checking out different parts of the coastline for possible landing sites. Our coastguard patrols are on the lookout for regular, known operations and boats which follow recognizable routes and patterns. The odd newcomer might easily slip through the net.'

Martin considered the argument, yet remained unconvinced. There was still one aspect of the puzzle which worried him. It was something he hadn't bothered to mention to Willerbey and Crewes, but he brought it up now.

'Maybe I'd go along with you – but for one thing,' he said. 'The reaction of the character left on the boat after my men attacked. It doesn't make sense. He made no attempt to investigate or mount any kind of rescue attempt for his two mates. He simply got the hell out, as fast as he could.'

Selina couldn't quite follow the argument through. 'So what are you suggesting?'

'That they were half expecting opposition – which in turn presupposes that they knew we were there,' Martin told her. 'All the man on the boat could see was a wrecked inflatable and two of his comrades floating in the water. It could have been a simple accident – in which case he would have tried to pick them up, surely? At the very least he should have been curious, or surprised. But his immediate reaction was all wrong.'

For the first time, Selina's personal conviction wavered. She frowned slightly as she ran Martin's argument through her mind.

'Maybe he just panicked,' she ventured. 'Maybe he could tell they were both dead – who knows? And maybe you're just trying to read too much into this whole thing.'

'And then again maybe there's something bloody

fishy about this entire incident which your people might have some ideas about,' Martin put in, capitalizing on the girl's moment of doubt. 'Worth at least trying to follow through, wouldn't you say?'

Selina was thoughtful for several more seconds, finally conceding the point with a vague toss of her head. 'OK, I'll check,' she said. 'But if you're looking for a weak link in the chain, might I suggest you look more to your own camp? Your tame Russian, for a start. What do you really know about him? A supposedly simple merchant seaman, who jumps ship in Copenhagen and demands political asylum in Great Britain. Perhaps a very convenient way for the KGB to insert a double agent?'

'That was three years ago,' Martin pointed out. 'Following which he was thoroughly debriefed by two separate branches of British Intelligence and every aspect of his story checked and double-checked. Since then he has given us invaluable information concerning the deployment of Soviet spy ships posing as fishing trawlers and factory ships – every detail of which has checked out one hundred per cent.' Martin broke off to shake his head vehemently. 'No, Pavlaski's straight, I'm sure of it.'

There was a look approaching hostility in Selina's eyes as she spoke again. 'It might be nice if you could credit me with the same degree of trust, Lieutenant-Colonel,' she said coldly. 'And now, if you'll excuse me, I have to start preparing breakfast for our guests. More like a woman's work, as I'm sure you agree.'

There was nothing else to say. Feeling uncomfortable, as he always did in the company of strong-minded females, Martin had no choice but to do something which went against every fibre of his being, and retreat in the face of the enemy.

10

'You've got to admit it's one hell of a fascinating design problem,' Jim Mallory said, peering over Bright's shoulder at some of the Englishman's preliminary sketches.

Bright started slightly. He'd been so engrossed in his work he hadn't heard Mallory enter the room. He turned and looked up with a surprised grin on his face. 'Oh yes, it's fascinating enough,' he agreed. 'But rather pointless, I can't help feeling. I mean, feasibility studies and concept designs are one thing. But producing anything practical out of it is something else.'

'Who knows? But as it's all Martin seems to want – for the moment, at least – we might as well enjoy ourselves. Hell, let's all take the money and run.'

'You sound almost disappointed,' Bright said, with slight surprise in his voice. 'I thought you were sceptical about the whole concept.'

'I guess I was,' Mallory admitted. 'But the more I think about it, the more enthusiastic I get. It would be one neat little machine.' He paused to study Bright's sketches more closely. After a while, he bent over and pointed to the rough design of the board itself. 'Ever considered the possibility of getting away from the single-hull concept?' he mused. 'Like twin outriggers, for instance?'

Bright frowned – partly because he bristled at the idea of other people telling him his job and partly because he couldn't see any point in such a suggestion. 'You mean something like a catamaran rig?' he said rather dismissively. 'It's already been thought of – and tried. Too unstable in rough water.'

Mallory wasn't going to be put off. He shook his head and picked up one of Bright's propelling pencils. 'No, I was thinking more in terms of two separate sections which would slot and lock together,' he said, doodling a couple of rough shapes on Bright's sketch pad.

Bright's eyes narrowed. 'What's the point of that?' he wanted to know.

Mallory looked a little sheepish. 'It would do me one hell of a favour,' he admitted. 'There's one little problem I can't see any other really efficient way around.'

He had Bright's interest now. 'What sort of a problem?'

Mallory came clean. 'I can design something which will get off the ground, and set it to fly at any height, and for whatever distance, Martin wants,' he explained. 'The sticky part comes in putting it down cleanly on the water again. It's a question of trim and balance.'

Bright suddenly thought he understood. 'So

you're thinking of two separate floats — like a seaplane?'

Mallory nodded. 'Something like that,' he agreed. 'But it would also help to give the vessel some stability in the water while the engine and extraneous parts were being dismantled. That in itself is going to be a tricky little problem that I bet nobody else has thought about.'

The American was probably right, Bright reflected. Thinking about it more carefully, it became clear just how much of a problem that part of the operation could be — especially in choppy water. He turned to a clean page in his sketch pad and roughed out a pair of thinner, slightly asymmetrical hull shapes. 'I suppose I could incorporate some kind of a locking assembly around the mast seating assembly without affecting the overall aquadynamics,' he said as he drew another quick but confident diagram. 'That the sort of thing you had in mind?'

Mallory nodded eagerly. 'Now you're cooking,' he said. 'And if the mast itself is assembled out of two identical lengths of tubing, then I'd have the bracing struts I need to stabilize the floats.'

Bright thought about that idea for a few seconds, before shaking his head. 'I'd rather you thought in terms of two curved bracing bars,' he said. 'That would then give me a quick and easy way to design the wishbone for the boom assembly. The mast would be better in one piece — perhaps serving its initial purpose as the central spine for your wings.'

Mallory's eyes were sparkling now. 'Yeah, no problem,' he said generously. He let out a little whoop of exhilaration. 'Jesus, Mike, we've almost cracked it.'

Bright grinned quietly to himself, not yet quite able to accept his colleague's somewhat naive dismissal of the countless technical problems still to be tackled. It was so typically American, he thought – that almost childlike sense of enthusiasm. It was something which Bright found quite appealing, although many of his countrymen often mistook it for brashness. He tried to bring Mallory back to reality as gently as he could.

'We're on the way, Jim, but there are still a few little bugs we need to iron out,' he reminded him. 'Like how your wings are going to convert into a sail for a start.'

It didn't dampen Mallory's eagerness for a second. 'Yeah, well that's your girlfriend's job, isn't it?' he pointed out. 'Don't you think maybe it's time we brought her in on this?'

Again the American was probably right, Bright realized. The entire operation was best tackled as a joint project, with everyone free to point out their particular problems and make suggestions as to how best to get round them. 'Maybe we'd also better bring Martin up to date with our ideas so far,' he added. 'After all, he's still the only person round here who really knows what this bloody contraption is actually for.'

Mallory was in full agreement. 'Good idea,' he said. 'You go find Janice and I'll see if I can track down Martin. We'll have a planning conference in the common room in half an hour.' He paused, eyeing Bright thoughtfully. 'While we're at it, how about your buddy Randy? Do we bring him in too?'

There was a slight edge to the question, Bright sensed. It was almost as if Mallory had some slight resentment, even suspicion.

'You don't seem too sure about Randy,' he pointed out, bringing it into the open.

Mallory looked a little awkward. 'Well, I guess I'm just not too sure exactly where he fits into this thing,' he admitted. 'I mean, where's his input supposed to come?'

It was a question which Bright hadn't yet figured out for himself, though he wasn't prepared to admit it to Mallory. 'Well, Martin obviously wants him involved,' he said, evading the issue. 'So I suppose we'd better include him in any discussions.'

'And the Russki?' Mallory asked, even more dubiously.

Bright shrugged. 'What would be the point? He hardly speaks any English. We can't even communicate with him.'

Mallory grunted sceptically. 'Or so he lets us believe,' he said sullenly. Maybe he understands a damn sight more than he lets on.'

Bright thought about the suggestion. Another stock American characteristic – an instinctive distrust of the Russians – he wondered. Or might Mallory have a valid point? Either way, it hardly mattered for the purposes of their current conversation. It was pretty clear that the consensus was to keep Pavlaski out of things unless Martin specifically ruled to the contrary.

Bright rose to his feet and picked up his sketch pad. 'All right, the common room in half an hour,' he said to Mallory, and left the room in search of Janice and Randy.

11

As promised, Selina had checked through her contacts with Greek Military Intelligence and the answer was negative. They had no knowledge of nocturnal activity in the area and were unable to offer any suggestions other than that they step up offshore patrols along that stretch of the coast for a few days. Martin had no choice but to accept, if not believe, this assessment. He did, however, politely but firmly decline the offer of increased surveillance. He needed greater secrecy, not less.

The mystery, and the doubt, remained. Having agonized over it for most of the morning, Martin finally decided to contact his own highest authority at top secret level. Two hours later he found himself speaking directly to no less a personage than the Foreign Secretary himself, on a priority hotline patched and scrambled through GCHQ in Cyprus.

'Are you asking me for permission to abort this mission?' asked the Foreign Secretary bluntly, after listening to Martin's briefing.

Martin thought carefully before answering. The man's attitude to the situation had slightly thrown him. He had been expecting more of a panic reaction, given the extremely sensitive nature of the project. Instead, it seemed that the Foreign Secretary wanted to play cat and mouse. Or perhaps it was simply the game of diplomacy.

'With respect, sir, I was merely attempting to sound out official reaction,' Martin replied warily. 'After all, if the integrity of this mission has been compromised, then there are almost sure to be severe political repercussions — and that's your department far more than it is mine.'

The sound that came back over the line could have been a cough or a short, dry laugh. 'I wouldn't necessarily say that, Lieutenant-Colonel Martin. You seem to have a fairly decent grasp of the principles involved.'

The Foreign Secretary paused, finally continuing on a more serious note. 'Do you honestly believe that the mission has been compromised?'

Put on the spot, Martin could only report the situation as he saw it. 'I really don't know, sir,' he admitted.

'Then let's proceed on the assumption that last night's unfortunate occurrence was an isolated incident with no real bearing on the issue,' the Foreign Secretary said. 'As I see it, there is absolutely no reason to curtail operations at this stage. You have your personnel in place, and we are still several weeks away from any more positive action. So why not carry through the next stage of the mission as planned?'

The suggestion made sense, Martin had to admit.

Scrapping the entire mission in response to a single unexpected incident did seem rather premature. And, as the Foreign Secretary had pointed out, they were still at the theoretical planning stage.

'And if there is any further trouble?' Martin asked. 'If there should be a leak in the near future?'

'Then we shall deny it vehemently, of course,' the Foreign Secretary said firmly. 'The British Government will stick to the original agreed cover story – that a task force of the Royal Marines was merely carrying out a feasibility study into the development of a new type of amphibious assault craft.'

'And you think the Russians will buy that?'

'I don't see they'll have any other choice, Lieutenant-Colonel. I'm quite sure we can handle any flak at diplomatic level. Whether the Russians choose to believe us or not, there will be no way they can prove otherwise.'

'Except through Pavlaski, of course,' Martin pointed out. 'My Greek Intelligence liaison officer has already suggested that he might be a double agent.'

There was a long, thoughtful sigh at the London end of the line. 'Yes, of course we are all aware of comrade Pavlaski's unique position,' the Foreign Secretary replied eventually. 'Not only is he absolutely crucial to this mission – he must also be seen as potentially its weakest link, and thus expendable should the balloon go up. That, of course, must be left to your discretion.'

'I understand, sir,' Martin muttered. There was

no need for the Foreign Secretary to further clarify the situation. 'So we proceed as scheduled?'

'Indeed,' the Foreign Secretary confirmed. 'But do keep me informed should there be any further developments. And please keep in mind that you have total discretion at all times, Lieutenant-Colonel. You are on the spot – I am not. Should you consider that further or emergency action is required at any time, that decision is purely yours. Do I make myself clear?'

'Absolutely, sir,' Martin said, grimacing. He replaced the receiver, shaking his head slowly from side to side. The final message had been clear enough – and exactly what he had expected. As usual, he was left holding the shitty end of the stick, and he would have to be damn careful that none of the crap stuck to his hands if he ever chose to throw it away.

Mallory was lurking in the hallway outside as Martin came out of the room he had adopted as his private office. The vague thought that the young American had been eavesdropping flashed through his mind, but he pushed it away. He was getting paranoid, he told himself.

'Can I do something for you, Mr Mallory?' he asked, slightly more curtly than he had intended.

'Actually, I thought you wanted me to do something for you,' came the reply. 'We think we might have come up with some workable initial design roughs and thought you might like to see them. We're having a conference meeting in the common room in about twenty minutes.'

Martin forced a look of enthusiasm on to his face. 'Good, I'll be there,' he said as brightly as he could manage. 'I'll be looking forward to seeing what you've all come up with.'

As Mallory was in charge of the first stage of the craft's functional life, it seemed only appropriate for him to open the discussion.

'Well, the general consensus is that this beast is at least theoretically possible,' he started, directing himself to Martin although he was addressing them all. 'I think I can make it fly, and Mike seems to feel he can come up with something which could be handled on the water once we set it down. We can both make design concessions which will allow us to duplicate certain key assembly parts – or at least make them convertible. The main drawback would appear to be how much of the original structure could actually be salvaged and used again. At the moment, it looks to me as though you would probably have to jettison up to seventy per cent of the original design and have to do a fair amount of amateur engineering work on the water before you could progress to stage two. It's going to be extremely wasteful in terms of materials, and time-consuming in making the adaptations.'

Martin didn't seem unduly worried. 'The amount of stuff we have to dump isn't really important,' he assured the meeting. 'Cost is not a major priority, and this craft is not expected to be reusable. Think of it as a strictly single-trip disposable.' He turned his attention to Mike Bright. 'Complicated conversion procedures on the water do bother me, however. How far do you think we might be able to simplify the process?'

Bright sucked at his teeth. 'This is really only our first serious look at the concept,' he conceded. 'But I'm pretty sure we can find ways to cut a few corners when we study the problems in greater depth.'

Martin seemed reasonably satisfied for the present. He glanced at Janice. 'Any real problems in your department, Miss Reece?'

The girl shook her blonde curls, smiling broadly. 'None at all. I seem to have the easy part. It's a fairly simple task to design the microlight wings as a series of interlocking, nylon-zipped panels which can simply be taken apart and put together again in a new configuration in a matter of seconds. It will create several weak stress-points, of course, although an overlapping seam fitted with a series of locking press-studs would help to minimize the risk of separation failure.'

Mallory took the opportunity to interrupt, voicing the major concern which had been bothering him from the start.

'Which brings us to the real crunch issue of safety,' he pointed out. 'The bottom line is that this machine is going to be, by definition, a whole series of compromises. Every single deviation from standard design is going to create a new area for potential failure or performance variation. To put it bluntly, Mr Martin, it's going to be a very dangerous and unpredictable bitch to fly. I just want you to be fully aware of that.'

Martin flashed the American an icy, cynical smile. 'Point taken, Mr Mallory. But let me assure you that we won't be taking any fare-paying passengers.'

'But someone is going to have to control this craft,' Bright put in. 'I think we've already established that this whole project is more than a theoretical exercise. Right, Lieutenant-Colonel?'

'Right,' Martin agreed with a brief nod. He saw no point in denying it any further.

'So this little hybrid is going to get built, and your men are going to be expected to control it?' Taking full advantage of Martin's sudden and uncharacteristic openness, Bright was determined to push the man as far as he was prepared to go.

This time Martin said nothing. Bright took his silence as an admission in itself. 'Then what Mallory said goes for my side of things as well,' he pointed out. 'This design is bound to be inherently faulted, with a performance which could be erratic, to say the least. Your men may have had plenty of experience sailing conventional windsurfers, but they will not be prepared to cope with a craft which will probably handle like this one will. She'll be sluggish in response, heavy as hell to handle in anything over a ten-knot wind and none too reliable.'

'I get the general picture,' Martin cut in, a trifle peevishly. 'But that's why Mr Havilland is with us. It will be his job to train my men in the handling of the first prototypes.'

The simple statement was like a bombshell. There followed several moments of stunned silence as the full implications of what Martin had said sank in with everyone present. It was Bright who found his voice first. He whirled on Martin, his tone a mixture of anger and incredulity.

'Are you telling us now that you expect us to actually build you a working prototype?' he demanded.

Martin's face was impassive. 'That would be the next stage of the operation, yes. But not one prototype. Five, to be exact.'

It was Mallory's turn to explode. 'You're crazy, man,' he blurted out. 'You told us we were only going to be here a couple of days at the most.'

Martin shook his head. 'No, Mr Mallory. What I said was that I estimated it would take you only a few days to decide if this idea was technically feasible. You all seem to have agreed on that already. So what I am saying now is that we proceed immediately to phase two. Each of your individual fees will be doubled in return for your continuing cooperation, and I can arrange for your belongings to be brought here from your respective hotels should you agree, as I sincerely hope you will.'

The first wave of shock had passed. Bright began to laugh. 'Mallory's right, Martin. You *are* crazy. We'd need proper workshops, engineering facilities, materials — a hundred and one specialist pieces of equipment. Just for my side of things alone I'd need a couple of vacuum-moulding tanks, chemical mixing vats, two pressure tanks and a laminating oven. Janice would need a full-sized sail loft, industrial stitching machines and all her materials.'

'Of course,' Martin said calmly. 'Please don't take me for a complete fool, Mr Bright. We did consider every aspect of the project before approaching you. Everything you need will be provided. As I said before, cost is not one of our prime considerations.'

'And working space?' Janice queried.

'There is a block of four remaining villas which are not presently in use,' Martin told her. 'The interior walls have already been knocked out, which should give you adequate space. Obviously, we will make any minor alterations you specify. We can start bringing materials and equipment in by sea just as soon as I have your approval.'

A long silence fell, in which Bright, Mallory, Janice and Randy exchanged a series of stunned glances. It was quite obvious that Martin was deadly serious, even though the project seemed totally insane.

'Well?' Martin asked after a while. 'Do I have your cooperation?'

'More to the point, do we have a choice?' Randy put in, expressing the doubt which had occurred to them all. 'I mean, if we say we're not interested, are you really going to let us just walk out of here?'

Martin allowed the ghost of a smile to flit across his face. 'We're not terrorists, Mr Havilland. None of you are prisoners of war, or anything like that.

The plain answer to your question is, yes, you are free to leave at any time should you wish to do so.'

'And what would happen to the project?' Bright asked. 'You'd just drop it, write off all your obvious planning and preparation?'

Martin's temporary smile faded. Grim-faced again, he shook his head slowly. 'No, I'm afraid not, Mr Bright. Without your help, we would be forced to try to formulate some sort of an alternative using our own, rather more limited resources. As I said before, this mission is of vital importance. Lives are at stake.'

'Lives would be at stake even with our help,' Mallory said quietly. 'The lives of your men. If we went ahead, the prototype would have to be field-tested at every stage of development. We'd be progressing by trial and error alone, fine-tuning as we went along. Are you and your men prepared for the risks that would entail?'

Martin nodded gravely. 'We are all aware of the dangers. And we know what will happen if we fail. On balance, it has to be worth any risks. We have no real choice.'

Silence fell again. Martin studied each of the faces in the room in turn, trying to gauge what thoughts were going on behind the bemused expressions. He was looking for hope, but could see only doubt. With a slightly sinking feeling, he realized that he was probably losing them, and wished there was something he could do about it. But there was nothing. His hands were tied. If only he could tell them what was at stake, he thought bitterly. If only they knew how many innocent civilians might die, what sort of a bloodbath might erupt in one of the most volatile flashpoints of the world. It was a pointless thought. His orders had been explicit and unequivocal. Absolute secrecy. Operation Windswept was probably the most sensitive mission he had ever been involved in, and any leak would have disastrous international repercussions. Even his own men were still in the dark about their actual mission, and could not be briefed before the project moved safely into phase two. Everything hung on the decision of four bewildered, dubious and uninformed civilians. Martin could only wait, in the hope that he had managed to convey to them all something of the sense of urgency he himself felt.

The mood was changing, slowly and very subtly. Glances became less inflexible, more questioning. Instead of mere doubt, the stirrings of curiosity showed themselves, in turn gradually hardening into a renewed sense of enthusiasm. The decision, when it was finally made, was somehow reached by mutual consent without a single word having been spoken. It appeared to be unanimous.

Mallory appointed himself spokesman. 'We still think this whole scheme is crazy,' he pointed out. 'But we'll build these contraptions for you.'

The relief on Martin's face was obvious. 'Thank you,' he said with genuine gratitude in his voice. 'I'll make the necessary arrangements right away to get things prepared for you. Perhaps you could all provide me with a full list of your most immediate requirements, and I'll get them ordered before the day is out.'

'This isn't going to happen overnight – you realize that?' Bright said. 'I don't know what sort of time-scale you had in mind, but this could take months.'

Martin faced him squarely. 'I told you I can get you anything you need, Mr Bright,' he said candidly. 'Everything except time. We have exactly seven weeks to get these craft built, tested and ready for action.' He paused, waiting for the expected chorus of protest, but it never came.

'Then we'd better get our asses into gear, right?' said Mallory, breaking the silence.

12

At last he could fully brief his men, Martin thought with a great sense of relief. Although many covert operations necessarily proceeded on a 'need to know' basis, it was somehow alien to SBS philosophy to keep Marines distanced from their commanding officers by a wall of secrecy – particularly in a tight, almost claustrophobic situation such as this. Not only did it tend to weaken the strong sense of comradeship and trust which was the very essence of the corps, it was not fair to the men themselves.

Every member of the SBS had proved himself to be a brave, strong and honest man. To deny them the full truth was a betrayal of those very qualities that made them so special. They deserved to know exactly what dangers they faced, and they deserved the right to prepare themselves for those dangers each in his individual way. As Martin so often reminded himself, the SBS were not supermen, and they were not, as some people imagined, beyond fear. The real difference was that they had trained themselves to live with it.

It was now early afternoon – the time when the

majority of the tourists would be packing into the tavernas and the native Greeks enjoying a siesta. Martin took a calculated risk in calling all his men back off perimeter and beach patrol so that he could address them as a team. This fact did not go unnoticed by the men themselves. There was an excited buzz in the briefing room as Martin finally prepared himself to outline their mission.

'Well, I suppose you know why I've called you all together,' Martin began.

'Yeah, you're going to tell us all a funny story, aren't you, boss?' Gareth Williams called out, winning a ripple of laughter from his comrades.

'Hope it's better than one of yours then, Taff,' Andy Donnelly put in. 'All your dirty jokes have sheep and wellington boots in 'em.'

This unashamedly racist dig was quickly followed by a chorus of further comments on the sexual orientation of Welshmen in general and Gareth in particular. Martin let it go, knowing that there was a slightly nervous edge behind the laughter and absolutely no malice in the mickey-taking. The good-natured banter was their way of releasing tensions before a major briefing. He waited until the men eventually settled down before continuing.

'You men were all hand-picked for this mission,' he went on. 'In case you hadn't figure it out for yourselves, the common link between you all is that each of you has had extensive experience of flying hang-gliders or microlight aircraft in addition to your training on all forms of water-borne craft.

Basically, this mission will rely very heavily on that experience.'

'So that's where the civvies come in, is it, boss?' Sooty put in. 'They're here to build us all one of those nice little James Bond chopper's that fit into a suitcase.'

Martin smiled. 'As it happens, trooper, you're closer to the truth than you think. As a matter of fact, they are designing a very special sort of flying machine for you men – but it's also a lot more.'

There were no further interruptions. Martin could see from the look on the Marines' faces that they were keen to get down to brass tacks.

'Anyway, the first thing I wanted to do was to apologize to you all for keeping this mission under wraps for so long,' he went on. 'The plain truth is that, owing to the extreme delicacy of the operation, it was impossible to release any details until I was sure we had secured the full cooperation of our civilian friends. I'm pleased to say that that hurdle is now cleared, and we have official approval to go ahead.' He paused briefly before going on. 'Some of you have probably wondered what you were doing playing nursemaids to a bunch of hippie types. Well don't let appearances fool you. Between them, our four guests represent possibly the finest and most innovative young designers in the West today. Their brief is to design and build a new kind of experimental multi-purpose craft which will be like nothing you have ever come across before. In that respect, gentlemen, you will all be guinea-pigs.'

'So we're going to be test pilots, eh, boss?'

Willerbey asked. 'Up there with the brilliantine and glory boys?'

Martin allowed himself a thin smile. 'Not quite, trooper. If I told you that Wilbur and Orville Wright would probably have turned this one down flat, you might have an idea of the risks involved. The nitty-gritty is that this machine will be the product of little more than a wild, perhaps even desperate, idea. It was conceived for this mission alone, although it is possible that it might, in the future, be developed into a completely new form of amphibious assault craft. For the moment, let me just tell you that it is basically a powered hang-glider which will convert into a seagoing sailing vessel. We'll get on to the specifics of design and application later. For the moment, I'd like to give you some of the background leading up to the mission itself.'

Martin broke off, striding across the room towards the display board mounted on one wall. He pulled down a rolled-up map and locked it into position. As he turned back to his men his face was set in a stony mask.

'From this moment on, gentlemen, may I remind you that this entire mission is of absolutely top-secret classification, priority one. Our code-name is Operation Windswept. Not a whisper of what I am about to tell you must be allowed to get outside the confines of this base – either before or after the actual operation.'

Under normal circumstances, the security of a mission briefing was taken for granted as an integral part of the job. The fact that the boss had seen fit to make special mention of it could only suggest that it was a matter of extreme and particular delicacy. This put many of the men on edge and provoked a buzz of speculation throughout the room.

Martin waited until everyone had settled down again before continuing. Ignoring the map for the moment, he concentrated on the basics of the situation.

'For some years now, the Russians have been supplying Syria – and we suspect Iraq too – with their SS21 missiles. With a range in excess of 9000 kilometres, multiple warheads and the capability to be launched from mobile stations, they represent the sharp end of current Soviet hardware and NATO have long considered them to be a particularly nasty threat in the already volatile Middle East. The only saving grace, to date, has been the fact that they were still operating on the traditional Soviet 'fly-by-wire' system originally developed for the earlier SS series back in the seventies. It had been generally held that the Western Alliance held the threat in check with the deployment of the American Patriot tactical air-defence system – which theoretically can out-manoeuvre, outfly and effectively neutralize just about anything else in the air.'

Martin stopped to take a deep breath. 'However, recent intelligence reports now indicate that we may have lost this very important tactical advantage, and I probably don't have to spell out what the possible repercussions could be.'

'You mean the Russkis have come up with a new missile we can't touch?' Williams asked.

'Not exactly,' Martin told him. 'And anyway, the sheer cost of replacing their existing SS21 systems would be far beyond the financial capabilities of most of their Middle Eastern customers. So basically the Soviets have come up with a compromise.'

Sooty let out a short, cynical laugh. 'The bastards are getting more like us every day, aren't they?' he said

'More than you know,' Martin agreed, with a nod. 'Not the least aspect of which is their increasing preoccupation with world trade. The Russians may well be muttering about *détente*, but it hasn't slowed down their increasing grip on international arms dealing. The SS21 has been the showpiece of their catalogue up to now, and they obviously can't afford to have it shown up. We now know that Soviet scientists have developed a new and highly sophisticated computer guidance system which can be fitted to existing SS21 installations.'

'You mean upgrade them?' Williams said.

'Worse than that,' Martin said, shaking his head gravely. 'If this new system is only half as good as our Intelligence boffins seem to think it is, then NATO forces have virtually no effective defence against it. It means that Syria and Iraq will shortly be able to put those bloody missiles just about any place they want to – and that places Israel right in the firing-line.'

Martin broke off to sigh heavily. 'Gentlemen, I don't have to spell out for you the possible consequences of a missile attack on that country. If, as we suspect, the Israelis already have some sort of limited nuclear capacity, nobody doubts that they would use it if their backs were really against the wall. A major Arab—Israeli war in the Middle East could have disastrous consequences for the Western powers – not the least of which would be total and possible long-term disruption of oil supplies.'

A ripple of excitement ran around the room. This was big-league stuff, and nobody present could fail to be totally awed by the implications.

'So where the hell do we fit into the big picture?' Sooty asked, speaking for them all.

It was a direct question, and it deserved a direct answer. Martin cleared his throat before continuing. 'Our mission is to steal one of these new guidance systems so that British and American scientists can come up with a workable countermeasure.'

There was a long, thoughtful silence before Bryan Bailey let out a slightly nervous giggle. 'Well, that's all right, then. Something nice and simple. We thought it might be a bit more complicated that that.'

The rest of the men took the opportunity to milk the situation for a little more tension-relieving humour.

'So what's the plan, boss?' Sooty asked. 'Do we paraglide into Red Square during one of the big parades and nick one off the back of a lorry?'

Willerbey had another suggestion. 'Perhaps we could just help ourselves to a complete missile and fly it home.'

Martin allowed himself a fleeting smile. 'Good ideas, gentlemen – but I think we'll stick with the original plan.' He was completely serious again. 'We have learned that the first consignment of these new guidance systems is due to be delivered to Syria in just under two months' time. They will be dispatched from the Black Sea port of Sebastopol on board a Russian cargo vessel, on a route which will bring it through the Straits of Bosporus and around the Turkish coast into the Mediterranean. Our task will be to intercept that vessel at a suitable point, board it, and steal one of the guidance systems.'

Colin Graham let out a long, low whistle. 'Jesus Christ, boss! You mean we're going to hijack a Russian ship?'

There was no point in trying to look for euphemisms. Martin nodded. 'That's about the size of it, yes.'

Graham shook his head from side to side in sheer disbelief. 'What the hell's in the minds of those guys at Ops? They want to kick off World War III or something?'

'Preferably not,' Martin said with massive understatement. 'Actually, the official view is that if we could get away with it, the Russians would simply be too embarrassed to let it go public. There would probably be a lot of angry muttering at diplomatic level, and then the whole business would die a natural death. They could be right.'

'Yeah, and they could be bloody wrong, too,' Sooty put in. 'We are talking about an act of piracy on the high seas, aren't we? Correct me if I'm wrong, boss, but isn't there some kind of international law about that?'

'Now you understand why this mission is so sensitive,' replied Martin.

It was another wild understatement, evoking a fresh wave of sarcasm from Sooty. 'So's the end of my prick,' he snorted. 'But I wouldn't use it to test the temperature of boiling water.' He fixed the CO with his eyes. 'Seriously, boss, do the boys in the back room really think we could get away with this caper? I mean, even if we managed to board this ship without getting bumped, how are we going to know where to go?'

Martin had an answer ready. 'That's where our Russian friend Pavlaski comes in,' he said quietly. 'Or rather, his intimate knowledge of the layout of Soviet commercial vessels. It will be his job to brief you all until you know the ins and outs of that ship like the back of your own hand. He will also be able to advise you on crew movements, watch patterns and the best places to run for cover if you have to. Once you get on board that vessel, you should have more than a fighting chance of grabbing one of those systems and getting clean away.'

'So how do we get to use this little magic carpet our civvy friends are cooking up for us?' asked Williams.

Martin picked up a pointer and turned to the map on the board, tracing it down the western coast of Turkey and around the south-western tip outside the Greek island of Rhodes. 'This, according to

Pavlaski, will be the route the ship follows,' he explained. 'Once in the Med, she'll come inshore again and hug the southern coast of Turkey all the way across to the Gulf of Iskenderun, where she'll drop down the Syrian coast to the port of Latakia. Our ideal attack point will be as she's about to pass between the Turkish coast and the north-eastern tip of Cyprus – around 320 nautical miles from this point. It's tricky water there and shipping usually slows down to a crawl, especially at night, which is when we'll be going in.'

Bailey had a question. 'Excuse me, boss, but why don't we intercept her closer to home? I mean, why not go in while she's still in the Aegean?'

'Good point, trooper,' Martin said. 'But there's one particularly good reason for that which will be explained later. For the moment, let's just say that there are certain . . . complications. On top of which, we have to pull you out again when it's all over – and that's going to be easiest and surest from a nice safe base like Cyprus.'

Martin moved the pointer back to the island of Samos. 'So, you will fly from here in the specially modified microlights to a point some fifty miles off the north-eastern tip of Cyprus,' he went on. 'Our designer friends suggest that this will be about the maximum range we can expect from this craft, and you'll still have somewhere safe to run in the event of the mission being aborted at the last minute or individual failure of any one of the craft. After landing on the water, the engine and much of the superstructure of the microlights will be jettisoned in the sea, and what remains converted into a crude but quite serviceable windsurfer. You will then sail to within interception point of the freighter under cover of dark, using passive night goggles, de-rig the sails and use the hulls as belly-boards to paddle in to the sides of the target. Comrade Pavlaski assures us that the stern of the vessel will be the most vulnerable. At that point you will attach yourselves and your boards to the hull with magnetic clamps, which will also serve as climbing aids so that one man can board the freighter and put over a rope for the rest.' Martin broke off, looking out over his men expectantly. 'Well, any more questions at this point?'

Sooty nodded. 'Just one,' he muttered. 'Why all this business with microlights and surfboards? Why can't we go in using conventional craft. Even a mini-submersible?'

Martin nodded thoughtfully. 'That brings me to the little complication I mentioned earlier,' he said. 'Our own intelligence – which is confirmed by Pavlaski's information – suggests that the Russians almost invariably protect sensitive cargoes like this with a naval military escort. It will be discreet, of course, operating under the pretence of legitimate military exercises, but it is almost certain that the freighter will be shadowed throughout its voyage by at least three patrol ships, fully equipped with state-of-the-art tracking and surveillance equipment. Going in silently, at night, under wind-power alone, represents our best chance of making a surprise raid. With luck, you can be off that freighter again before the shadowing naval patrol knows what's going on.'

'What about tracking the ship in the dark?' Willerbey asked. 'Even with PNGs, it's going to be like looking for a needle in a very big haystack.'

Martin smiled. 'The Greek authorities are helping us out on that one,' he said confidently. 'Since it is impossible to negotiate the Aegean and stay in international waters, the Russian ship is going to have to stray into Greek territorial water. This will provide a perfectly reasonable excuse for a Greek coastguard vessel to approach the freighter close enough to plant a small homing transmitter on the hull. It will be pre-set to a very specific tight-band frequency that the Russian naval vessels are highly unlikely to notice, even if they pick it up accidentally. That should take care of any tracking problems.'

It solved the problem right enough, Willerbey thought. But there was still one thing he didn't fully understand. 'Why should the Greeks be so willing to help us?' he asked. 'They usually take a pretty low profile on anything which might have international repercussions.'

Martin grinned. 'A favour owed,' he muttered. 'The Greek islanders – and particularly the residents of Samos – have links with the SBS which go back a long way. Right back to 1941, in case you don't know your history.' He turned his attention back to the rest of the men. 'So, that's just about it for now. Obviously we'll discuss a more concerted plan of attack for once you board the freighter at a later

112

date – after Pavlaski has briefed you all on layout and crew deployment. Thank you, gentlemen.'

The ensuing silence, as Martin gathered together his notes, gave everyone a chance to air their particular assessment of the operation.

'Well, you did warn us it was a wild scheme, boss,' Sooty put in. 'But I've got to admit – it's so bloody crazy it might just work.'

'A beautiful irony, too,' Bailey pointed out. 'The sheer gall of putting some crude, botched-up, wind-powered contraption up against the ultimate in high-tech computer surveillance systems. It's a work of sheer bloody art.'

Martin was in full agreement. 'Something our glorious founder would have been proud of,' he said, referring to the guiding light behind the formation of the original Special Boat Sections of the Army Commandos, direct forebears of the modern SBS. 'In fact, his legendary motto could have been coined specifically for this mission. "Excreta Tauri Astutos Frustrantur".'

The comment provoked a belly-laugh all round. Every SBS man was familiar with the story of how Roger Courtney had approached a Classics don at Oxford for a motto which would sum up the whole ethos of his fledgling unit. The result, sounding extremely impressive in the original Latin, had a very simple, very direct, translation: 'Bullshit Baffles Brains'.

As Martin had so wisely pointed out, it fitted their current mission as comfortably as a favourite old sock.

13

With the preliminary briefing of his men out of the way, and the enthusiastic cooperation of his civilian volunteers assured, Lieutenant-Colonel Martin felt a little happier. He felt quietly confident that he had managed to make the briefing itself as upbeat as possible, and had not conveyed to his men any of his personal misgivings about the mission.

Much as he tried to analyse his own feelings, Martin was still unsure about the true basis for his doubts, or indeed what those doubts actually were. It was surely not the concept of the microlight/surfboard itself, he rationalized to himself. The use of unconventional and experimental craft was probably the oldest tradition of the SBS, if not the actual basis on which it had been founded. From the Folboat canoes of World War II, the men of the Special Boat Squadron had acted as guinea-pigs for any number of bizarre maritime experiments, from riding the manned submersible torpedoes with detachable warheads nicknamed 'chariots' to being sealed alive within the claustrophobic nightmare of the early 'sardine can' one-man submarines.

Compared to that, piloting a 'flying surfboard', as Bright had described it, seemed almost tame.

Nor were the SBS strangers to operations of a sensitive political nature. In fact, the vast majority of their missions were conceived and executed in such complete secrecy that, for official purposes at least, they were deemed to have never happened. So it was certainly not that aspect of Operation Windswept which Martin found disquieting.

As for the more direct risks involved, the plan was dangerous, but hardly suicidal. When the time for the final briefing came, Martin was perfectly clear about what his orders would be. Direct engagement with Russian military personnel was to be avoided at all costs. There would be no shooting, for it would be made physically impossible. Apart from carrying a small amount of plastic explosive for blowing security bulkheads or hatch doors, his men would go in unarmed. It was one little detail of the operation which he had continued to withhold from them, and he was fully aware that they would be far from happy about it, but it was for their own protection as much as for diplomatic reasons.

Britain could ill afford direct confrontation with the Soviet navy, and the rest of the world would never sanction the murder of innocent Merchant Marine personnel – of any nationality. Nobody in official circles had been quite sure about what the current Soviet penalty for international piracy was, but it seemed unlikely that any of the men would be executed if they were unfortunate enough to be captured. It seemed far more likely that the

Russians would attempt to cover the whole thing up by clapping them in the Lubyanka. After that it would be up to the diplomats to sort out some kind of a deal behind the scenes.

With this final thought, Martin forced himself to think more positively, to concentrate on the many preparations which still had to be made. Whatever it was about Operation Windswept that was bothering him, it was little more than pure intuition, and far too vague and ill-defined to waste time worrying about. If something more tangible finally did surface from his subconscious, he would face it then, and make whatever decisions seemed appropriate at the time.

For the rest of the day he busied himself organizing the delivery of the most important items of equipment and materials on the list which Mallory, Bright and Janice had given him. That evening he ate alone in his room and assigned himself to night-time guard duty on the beach patrol. He was fully prepared for further trouble, but the night passed quietly, with no more nocturnal incursions into the bay.

Perhaps it had been no more than an isolated event, quite coincidental, he found himself thinking, as the brilliant dawn sun came up over his left shoulder, turning the surface of the sea to liquid fire.

14

Selina woke the CO at midday, with a light brunch of pitta bread, hummus and feta cheese salad – and the message that Bright and Mallory wanted to see him in the common room at his earliest convenience.

Martin propped himself up on his single pillow, cradling the breakfast tray across his lap. He looked up at Selina questioningly.

'How do they seem today, our civilian guests?'

The girl's dark eyes flashed with amusement. 'Excited, like little boys with a new toy,' she told him. 'You seem to have captured their imaginations with this little project of yours – whatever it is for.'

The short rider at the end of the statement was a covert attempt to elicit information, but Martin was astute enough to realize that more than mere curiosity was involved. He ignored it. 'Perhaps you'd be good enough to tell them I'll be with them in about half an hour,' he said, starting to tuck into his food.

Selina showed no sign that she was in any way disappointed. She was good, bloody good, Martin reminded himself. He wondered briefly just how much of the mission she had already pieced together for herself. She would be aware of the cooperation of the Greek Coastguard Authority in tagging the Russian freighter, of course – and there was no way of knowing how much information she might have prised out of Pavlaski.

Much depended on what actual brief her Greek Intelligence bosses had given her. Although her presence had been a prerequisite of the cooperation agreement, Martin suspected that her role was more that of an observer than a proper spy. Indeed it was more than likely that the Greek authorities didn't really want to know too much detail, for their own protection. The less they actually knew, the easier it might be for them to extricate themselves from an embarrassing situation if the shit hit the fan. As Corporal Willerbey had pointed out, the Greeks were not particularly noted for their willingness to get involved with international politics.

It was not worth worrying about, Martin decided. He finished his meal, rose, had a quick shower and shave and got dressed before going to join Bright and Mallory. As Selina had said, both men appeared to be in high spirits.

'You've made a bit of progress, I take it?' Martin asked.

Mallory grinned at him, pride showing on his face. 'Damn right,' he said emphatically. 'The more I think about this baby, the better she gets. We've even come up with a few ideas that should particularly please you.'

'Such as?'

Mallory picked up a sheaf of his latest design sketches from the nearby table. 'Remember you were concerned about radar surveillance?' he said. 'Well, we may have solved that particular little problem.'

The young man's enthusiasm was infectious. Martin felt a growing sense of excitement as Mallory began to expound on his ideas.

'The conventional microlight is built with an aluminium tube frame and steel cable rigging wires,' Mallory explained. 'Mainly for the sake of safety, durability and rigidity in rigging and de-rigging the wings. But of course for a strictly one-trip disposable craft, we don't really need any of those things. Once I realized that, of course, it opened up a whole new way of looking at this thing, and a completely different approach to construction and materials.'

'So what are you actually telling me?' Martin asked.

'That I can build this bird using nylon tubing, carbon fibre and Kevlar,' Mallory said proudly. 'Apart from the small engine and a few bolts and bracing struts, it can be more or less metal-free — thus virtually no radar trace.'

The American had been right, Martin thought. It *was* good news — although there was one minor problem.

'It's a great idea,' he said warmly. 'But what about when the microlight assembly is dismantled? Plastic isn't going to sink, and I'm not too keen on the idea of a load of tell-tale debris left floating about on the water.'

Mallory frowned slightly. It was something he hadn't even considered. He thought about it now for a few moments. Then his face brightened. 'No problem,' he announced with a grin. 'We simply lash all the extraneous parts to the engine housing. The weight of that alone should take everything to the bottom.'

It was a crude but effective solution to the problem, which Martin accepted. He turned his attention to Bright. 'How's the second stage working out?'

Bright was as optimistic as his colleague. 'Great,' he said, without reservation. 'No problems at all with the functional side of things, and like Jim said, by applying a little lateral thinking there's several things we can do to make the windsurfer as inconspicuous as possible.'

'How inconspicuous?'

Bright grinned. 'How about damn near invisible?' he asked. 'From aerial surveillance, at least.' He broke off to eye Martin curiously. 'I assume that somebody might be looking for these things from the air?'

Martin smiled faintly. 'They might,' he conceded. 'So how do you propose to overcome that potential problem?'

Bright shrugged. 'Designers have always made windsurfers bright and colourful because that's the way the customers want and expect them,' he explained. You need something different – you can have it. There's no reason at all why I can't form the hull out of perfectly clear polyurethane. Janice can make the wings and sail out of transparent plastic sheeting. It's not the most robust of materials, but it's more than adequate for one trip. With the boom, mast and your men's wetsuits in a nice neutral blue, they'd be near impossible to spot from anything but a very low-flying and very slow plane.' Bright paused. 'Oh, and I came up with one other nice little gimmick to help fool anyone who might want to take a more careful look.'

Martin was already impressed. Now he was intrigued. 'Let's hear it.'

'No matter how well the craft is camouflaged, anything moving across the surface of the water is going to leave a wake,' Bright explained. 'Seen from an aircraft, they're unmistakable. Your men might as well leave a trail of smoke flares behind them.'

It was something Martin had never thought about. He cursed himself mentally for the oversight. 'And you think you can get around that?'

Bright nodded. 'To an extent, yes. The problem is with the dagger-board, or keel. It not only stabilizes the board – it keeps it in line, thus creating a prefectly straight, unbroken wake trail. I plan to fit a couple of smaller spoiler fins to the rear underside of the hull. They shouldn't affect the handling characteristics too much, but they will help to break up the wake trail into more irregular swirls. Four of them in a line could easily be mistaken for a pod of dolphins or something like that.'

Bright looked proud of himself. As well he might,

Martin thought, with such an ingenious solution to a problem he hadn't even known existed. He looked at Bright with undisguised admiration. 'Any other little brainwaves?'

Bright smiled. 'Just one. I was thinking about incorporating an emergency flood chamber into the hull. Just in case anyone came too close, your men could simply pull the plug and sink the entire craft to about three feet below the water level. Then, when the danger had passed, they would blow out the water ballast with a compressed-gas cartridge, replace the plug and be on their merry way again. It would only work once – but that might be the one chance you needed.' He broke off, staring Martin in the eye. 'Well, what do you think?'

Martin wasn't very good at handing out compliments. 'Just do it,' he said. He was at something of a loss for further words. 'How soon do you think we can get down to a final design?' he asked finally.

Bright and Mallory exchanged a quick glance.

'Just as soon as you're prepared to give us the rest of the information we need,' Mallory said. 'I need the weight of each pilot, and we could both do with a fairly accurate idea of your final destination.'

Martin was immediately cagey. Up to that point everything had been going even better than he could have expected. Now he found himself back on potentially treacherous ground again, and he was far from happy about it. 'Why do you need that information?' he asked warily. 'I've already made it clear that there are certain specific details of this project which I am not at liberty to reveal.'

Mallory spoke with exaggerated patience. 'Think about it, man,' he urged. 'I have to work out payload and range.' He paused to let the point sink in. 'And it would be a great advantage if we had some sort of an idea what wind and weather conditions to plan for.'

Martin took the point, albeit grudgingly. 'The weight of the pilots is no problem,' he said. 'I'll have that for you by this evening. As far as destination is concerned, let's just say somewhere around Cyprus, for the sake of argument.'

It was obviously the nearest thing to a precise answer he was likely to get, Mallory decided. In the absence of hard facts, it would have to do. He wondered momentarily how the man would react to the one delicate question which was still bothering him. 'There is one last thing,' he said. 'There isn't going to be any leeway for undisclosed factors on my final calculations. So if you're planning any extra cargo you haven't told us about, you'd better come clean now.'

Martin looked, and sounded, a little indignant. 'I'm not sure I understand what you are suggesting,' he protested, almost pompously.

Mallory's lips curled in a thin, mirthless smile. 'Cut the crap, Martin,' he said wearily. 'We both know these little beauties aren't being built for your men to enjoy some R and R. So if you have any plans to increase your baggage allowance – with mines, some sort of warhead or any shit like that – this is your last chance to tell us about it right now or forget it. The payload of these birds is going to be strictly limited, and totally inflexible.'

It was the last hurdle to cross, Martin realized. He looked Mallory straight in the eye, his face devoid of any guile. 'You have my word that my men will be carrying no armaments of any kind,' he said quietly and sincerely.

The American returned Martin's gaze for several seconds, finally nodding thoughtfully. 'OK, that's good enough for me,' he said. 'Who could doubt the word of an English officer and gentleman?'

Martin could not mistake the sarcasm in this last comment, but he chose to ignore it. 'Well, it would appear that we have all systems go,' he observed, genuine satisfaction clearly registering in his tone. 'The equipment and supplies you wanted are already on their way. Please let me know if there is anything else you require.'

Mallory grinned at him. 'Yeah, you could try being human a bit more often. Believe it or not, it suits you.'

15

'Well, what do you think?' Willerbey asked Crewes as they headed from the villas down towards the beach to take up the late-afternoon patrol duty.

The man had been oddly withdrawn all day, Crewes thought. It wasn't like him, and it caused Crewes to consider his reaction. His initial response was an attempt at humour – he let out something between a grunt and a snort of derision. 'We don't get paid to think,' he replied. It was not the right thing to say. He caught a glimpse of the doubtful frown which flickered across Willerbey's face and relented. 'What do I think about what, anyway?' he added, after a few seconds.

'This bloody mission,' Willerbey said. 'Does it sound like a real shitter to you – or what?'

Crewes eyed his partner warily. Martin's orders to treat the operation as a matter of the highest possible security had been clear enough. However, they didn't specifically rule out discussing it among themselves, within the confines of the base. Although it was a practice which was certainly not encouraged within the SBS, it wasn't actually forbidden.

He shrugged non-committally. 'Been on worse,' he said, picturing in his mind the nightmarish landing on South Georgia two years earlier in which he had witnessed three out of five Gemini assault craft containing his comrades swept away by howling winds into a freezing hell of pack ice and thundering water. That was followed by three days of living rough and hiding out in a near-Arctic wasteland, knowing that you were outnumbered at least seven to one, and the enemy were all around you. After an experience like that, just about anything seemed comparatively tame. Crewes shuddered slightly at the memory before snapping back to reality – a tremor which did not go unnoticed by his companion.

'You got bad vibes about this one too?' Willerbey asked almost eagerly.

Crewes felt a little sheepish. 'No, no,' he protested with false bravado. 'I was thinking of something else, that's all.' He stopped in his stride, looking at Willerbey with a slightly puzzled expression. He'd known the man for three years, and had never seen him so unsure of himself. 'What the hell's got into you, anyway? You're acting like a virgin in a whorehouse.'

The man gave a sad, wistful smile. 'Tell you the truth, I just don't bloody well know. Just a feeling I can't quite shake off. Fucking weird.'

Crewes thought he understood. 'Are you still worrying about those two bandits we topped the other night?'

'A bit,' Willerbey admitted candidly. 'But it's

more than that.' He caught the strange expression which flickered momentarily across Crewes' face and recognized it as embarrassment with something of a shock. He forced a grin on to his face. 'Oh, shit, I must be getting soft in my old age.'

The matter dropped right there. 'Which side of the beach do you fancy?' Willerbey asked, quickly changing the subject.

Crewes shrugged. 'I'm easy. I'll take the far end if you like.'

Stepping on to the shingle, Crewes began to trudge up towards the headland, not sorry to be alone again. He found Willerbey's strange mood quite unnerving, for it struck uncomfortable chords in his own mind. Killing the man in the inflatable had not caused him a single second of anguish or self-doubt. He'd been given orders, and he'd followed them. He felt no sense of personal responsibility for causing the man's death, and that was the bit which bothered him now. Perhaps he *should* feel something, Crewes thought to himself. Willerbey had made him look into the dark mirror of his own conscience for a moment, and it was disconcerting to realize that there was no reflection at all.

Willerbey watched his companion walk away up the beach for a few moments before turning in the opposite direction and falling into a steady pace along the water's edge. He too was now glad for the solitude, feeling that he had somehow made a fool of himself in his fellow trooper's eyes. Besides, it would give him a chance to analyse his own thoughts more clearly, and try to pin down the odd sense of depression which had affected him ever since Lieutenant-Colonel Martin's briefing.

It wasn't fear, of that he was perfectly sure. Fear was natural – even healthy – and it could even be turned to positive advantage. The confused feelings which bothered him now were decidedly unhealthy, lurking below the surface like the first symptoms of a disease about to erupt. At the very heart of the matter, it was probably that he distrusted peacetime missions, Willerbey told himself. And a peacetime mission which involved civilians was even worse. Inexplicably, the word 'dishonourable' sprang into his mind, along with a whole set of negative emotions.

A war situation was something else. There was something essentially honest about war. You knew exactly who your enemy was, and he accepted you as his. You were both trained, professional soldiers – not only aware of the risks, but prepared for them, accepting them as part of the job.

And in his own case, that was a job taken by choice, for a specific reason. Willerbey was no secondary school drop-out, lured into the local army recruitment office by poor qualifications and a lack of drive. He'd left grammar school at seventeen with five GCEs, having seriously considered the possibility of A levels and then university.

The armed services had been chosen not as a job, but as a career. A chance to serve the country he loved, and believed in. Admittedly the army had not been his prime ambition. Willerbey's first choice had been to join the Royal Air Force as a pilot training officer. He'd more than made the grade on the entrance examinations, and would have been considered prime officer material if a poor colour-perception rating had not let him down. Medically unfit for aircrew membership, he'd been forced to rethink his position, finally deciding that if he couldn't fly then there was nothing else in the RAF he wanted to do.

Although offered Willerbey's services by default, the army had been grateful to recruit this potential officer, and he was accepted into service, eventually taking up a posting to the Royal Marine Commandos. He became a corporal shortly before his twentieth birthday and a year later applied to go on the SBS Potential Recruits' Course at Royal Marines, Lympstone, Devon. Sheer guts and determination pulled Willerbey through the three gruelling weeks of selection and testing, which were followed by nearly three months of intensive training in all forms of seamanship and a range of specialist skills which included diving, underwater demolition work, close-quarters combat and handling a wide variety of explosive and special weapons.

Two months later, after jungle warfare training in Brunei and a four-week parachute course, Willerbey was entitled to wear the trophies of his ordeal in the form of the legendary green beret and the two badges of parachuting wings and the 'Swimmer Canoeist' (SC) emblem to adorn the right-hand shoulder and forearm of his Royal Marines uniform. Corporal Simon Willerbey was finally an SBS Marine, just as the Argentinians were preparing themselves to invade the coveted Malvinas Islands.

The Falklands War threw Willerbey in at the deep end, and somewhat to his surprise he found that he liked the water. To say that he enjoyed his first taste of war was not strictly true. Killing did not come easily to him, or sit lightly upon his conscience, but he fought with a sense of pride and dedication which was a source of pleasure in itself. In the brief and bloody weeks which followed, he truly discovered his own complicated self and found that he was one of a rare and strange breed of man. He was a soldier who loved soldiering and was totally committed to the job, although the ethics of warfare would continue to disturb and bother him.

The intervening two years had been both a relief and a disappointment to him. He had spent much of his time enrolling for every new special-skills course and continuation-training programme going. The rest he dedicated to the one love which had never left him – the thrill of flying – and it was his vast experience of every form of aerial sport from free-fall parachuting to hang-gliding which had assured him his place on Samos, as part of the Windswept team.

The crackling roar of powerful twin turbo-fan aero engines snapped Willerbey out of his reveries. He looked up and to his right as the jet fighter seemed to materialize out of a cloudless sky, streaking almost vertically towards the surface of the Aegean before flattening out at about three hundred feet and banking on to a course which would bring it straight along the coastline. The screaming of the engines rose in pitch to a shuddering whine as the aircraft streaked along the beach and almost directly over Willerbey's head. Reaching the headland, it banked once again out over the sea and began to rotate into a steep climb. Moments later, as it dwindled to a mere speck in the sky, Willerbey heard the double crack of the engines' afterburners cutting in, followed some thirty seconds later by a duller explosion as it accelerated past Mach 1 and sent the boom of its supersonic footprint reverberating across the sounding board of the sea.

Lieutenant-Colonel Martin was running from the villas down toward the shoreline, gazing helplessly up into the empty sky.

'What the hell was that?' he called to Willerbey.

Willerbey was in no doubt at all, having recognized the aircraft immediately by its outline alone. Planes remained one of his enduring hobbies, and he was virtually a walking *Jane's Guide*. 'French-built Dassault Super Mirage Delta, sir,' he told his CO. 'Built for the export market as a long-range combat fighter specially designed for low-altitude penetration attack.'

If Martin was impressed by Willerbey's fund of aviation information, he didn't show it. 'Then what the fuck was a French plane doing here?' he barked.

'It could have come from anywhere,' Willerbey, replied calmly: 'The frogs have never been too fussy about who they sell arms to. Various versions of the Mirage are in service with well over a dozen countries throughout the world.'

But with one notable exception, Martin realized with something of a shock. He was no match for Willerbey when it came to identifying individual aircraft, but he had a pretty extensive knowledge of strategic arms deployment in both Western and Eastern Europe. 'But not, to the best of my knowledge, with the Greek Air Force,' he said pointedly. 'So what the bloody hell was it doing in Greek airspace? More to the point, what was it doing here?'

He turned to Willerbey with an afterthought. 'I suppose you didn't spot any markings?' he asked hopefully.

Willerbey shook his head. 'Sorry, boss. She went almost directly over my head. I only saw the underside of the wings and belly. Besides, it only made the one quick pass – if indeed it was a pass at all.'

'What else could it have been?' Martin asked suspiciously. The plane overflying this particular section of the island coastline was another mystery.

Willerbey thought for a few seconds before offering alternative explanations. 'The pilot could have had engine trouble at high altitude,' he suggested. 'Maybe one of his engines flamed out or something. He certainly came down in one hell of a dive before flattening out. That's a pretty common trick to kick an engine back on line. Mind you, I'd have thought any pilot worth his salt would have tried a stunt like that well out over the open sea.'

Martin had already come to the same conclusion. In the absence of any other plausible explanation, he could only assume that the plane had deliberately overflown the cove.

But what had the pilot thought he might see? Martin's brain screamed. The question only served to raise another, and much more important one. If Windswept was as secret as it was supposed to be, then why the hell had anyone come snooping around in the first place?

16

For several hours Martin agonized over whether or not to report the latest apparent incursion to the Foreign Secretary.

'Keep me informed should there be any further developments,' the man had said. But then he had also told Martin he had full discretion – effectively passing the buck straight back. It was a tough call, Martin felt. Any decision he made more or less hinged on his personal interpretation of the incident. Could the mysterious, but quite possibly coincidental, appearance of an unknown plane really be called a 'development'?

There was the panic factor to consider, also. The whole concept of the operation was already regarded as highly sensitive in government circles, and his last call would have done nothing to raise official confidence in the mission. Another negative report could well trigger a knee-jerk reaction which would result in someone pulling the plug, with all the consequences that might unleash. The Western powers would lose their one chance of getting their hands on the Russian missile-guidance system and the possibility of a disastrous flare-up in the volatile

Middle East would take a sudden and lurching step forwards. Within a couple of months the Syrians, and perhaps the Iraqis too, would have the capability of launching a major offensive against Tel Aviv. As the Foreign Secretary had already chillingly spelled out, the repercussions of such an attack could easily affect the whole world.

Martin was also honest enough with himself to consider the possibility of overreaction on his part. Looking at it coldly and objectively, what did he actually have? Two mysterious incidents, either of which might have been purely accidental and which might or might not be connected. Given the fact that the operation itself was still barely out of the planning stage, it gave only the thinnest excuse for reaction at all, let alone a reason to abort such a vitally important mission.

Finally, after much deliberation, Martin decided to take the Foreign Secretary at his word and exercise his own discretion. With that decision made, and the full burden of responsibility firmly shouldered, there remained the question of what he was going to do about it.

Martin let his mind go into free, unassociated thought. It was a trick he had learned many years ago, and frequently resorted to when he had to consider any particularly complex problem, or a situation in which there were no clear, unequivocal factors. A form of parallel thinking, it enabled him to mentally step outside facts – or the lack of them – and review the situation in holistic terms. Sufficiently detached, he could process the most complex problem in terms of a series of 'ifs' which might be independent or related.

This technique quickly unmasked the single key point on which everything else hinged. The Samos base was either being spied upon or it was not. If not, then the two mysterious incidents had no significance and were unrelated. Operation Windswept proceeded as planned, and the problem solved itself. At a single stroke, Martin had reduced his worries, and his field of consideration, by a straight fifty per cent.

The alternative viewpoint – that the operation was indeed under some kind of surveillance – could also be broken down into two distinct and separate possibilities. Either someone knew what they were looking for or they were simply looking for something. On the surface, that might seem to be an extremely subtle distinction to make, but it carried much deeper and more vital significance. If the former were true, then the whole operation was already compromised, and probably past salvaging. The second scenario was more hopeful, offering the distinct possibility that there might still be time to initiate some sort of a damage-limitation exercise or put up an effective smokescreen around the exact nature of Windswept.

But which of the two was most likely? Martin asked himself. He considered the matter gravely for several minutes, reviewing each possibility in turn.

On balance, it appeared almost impossible that any specific details of the plan could have leaked to an outside source. His own men had only been fully briefed earlier that day, and no one had left the complex. Up to that point, Martin himself had been the only person outside the confines of Whitehall who knew the exact nature of the mission, and he had confided in nobody. If any leak had already occurred, then it could only have come from British government sources themselves, and that was unthinkable.

All things considered, it appeared highly probable that there was no leak, and that sudden activity around the previously abandoned complex had merely aroused curiosity in some quarter. Someone, somewhere, had got a sniff that there was something going on, and was making tentative moves to find out what it was. The question of who that someone might be was a tantalizing one, but hardly relevant at that point, Martin decided. Identifying the most likely contenders could probably be achieved by a fairly simple process of trial and error, starting with the most likely. With this thought in mind, he began to run through the outlines of a plan which he had already begun to formulate in his mind. If he could work out the details, it was possible that he could kill two birds with one stone.

Martin was still not fully convinced that Selina was as totally innocent as she claimed, or that the Greek Intelligence Services were remaining quite as detached as they had promised. Which made them the number one suspect, he reasoned. It also simplified the formulation of his contingency plan.

Ten minutes later, Martin had it all worked out

in his head. A two-pronged plan, it should be as effective as it was simple. Resolved to put it into operation as soon as possible, he went in search of Selina.

The girl was not in the kitchen, nor in the common room. Excusing himself to Bright and Mallory, who were engaged in creating three-dimensional CAD designs on the computer, Martin headed for Selina's private quarters. He tapped gently on her door.

There was a longish pause before he received an answer. Martin imagined that he heard a brief exchange of muted voices, and the sounds of some rapid tidying up from inside the room. Finally came the rattle of the lock being turned and the door opened a few inches.

Selina peered out, looking slightly surprised to see him. She hesitated before opening the door any wider. 'Lieutenant-Colonel Martin, is there some sort of a problem?' she asked.

'Sorry to bother you,' Martin said, feeling that some apology was merited. 'It's just that something rather urgent has just come up, and I need to talk to you. Can I come in, do you think?'

The girl looked dubious for a second, then opened the door reluctantly.

Martin stepped into the room, and was immediately embarrassed. Randy Havilland lay sprawled on Selina's bed, an awkward grin on his face. Martin felt the heat of a flush spreading across his face. 'Look . . . I'm sorry . . . I didn't realize . . .' he began to stammer, avoiding Selina's eyes.

Randy swang his legs lazily over the edge of

the bed and rose to his feet. 'It's all right,' he said easily. 'We were just talking. Unfortunately,' he added, with a rueful smile. He looked over at Selina. 'Look, I'd better go. Perhaps I can see you later this evening?'

The girl nodded. 'Perhaps,' she murmured non-committally. She waved Martin over to a hard-backed chair as Randy let himself out of the room and closed the door. 'So what's the problem this time? That plane, I suppose? I can tell you right now that I have no more idea of where it came from than you do.'

Martin shook his head. 'It's not that specifically I needed to talk to you about. Something a bit more general, actually.' He sat himself down before continuing. 'To tell you the truth, I could do with your help.'

'But of course, that's what I'm here for,' Selina said immediately, looking and sounding perfectly genuine. 'What is it you think I might be able to do for you?'

There was no point in beating about the bush, Martin realized. 'Basically, I need a good cover story. A good, plausible reason to be here, and something which is fairly high-profile, so that we can be clearly seen to be doing something if anyone comes sniffing round. Apart from which, my men are getting bored, and that's not good for morale. They need something to keep them busy.'

Selina eyed him suspiciously. 'Why come to me?'

I thought there might be some little job we could

help your people out with. Do you a favour at the same time as I sort out my little problem.'

Martin watched Selina's face carefully, looking for her reaction and hoping to get some sort of an answer to at least one of his questions. If she seemed unwilling to cooperate, it might hint that she had something to hide. A direct refusal would almost certainly suggest that the Greek authorities were more deeply involved than he had been led to believe.

The girl merely looked thoughtful. 'Yes, I can see your point,' she said after a while. 'Anything specific in mind?'

Martin shook his head. 'Not really. I thought I'd leave that up to your people to decide. There must be something we could help them out with for a couple of weeks. Even a bit of coastal surveillance – if someone's willing to make a suitable boat available.'

'Yes, I'm sure there is,' Selina agreed with a brief nod. She considered the matter for a few seconds more. 'Look, I'll have a word with them first thing in the morning and see if they can come up with something.' She gave Martin a slightly apologetic smile. 'That's about the best I can do, at such short notice.'

'Yes, of course,' Martin said, slightly disappointed that he had actually learned nothing new. Selina was either an even better operative than he had already given her credit for, or she was one hundred per cent genuine. He could only wait and see which proved the most likely. He rose from his chair, there being little else to say. 'Well, I'll leave it with you,' he said by way of parting.

Selina escorted him to the door, flashing him a curious, almost defensive smile as he was about to leave. 'Oh, by the way, Randy and I *were* just talking, in case you're still wondering.'

She seemed particularly anxious that he should believe her, Martin thought. Was it natural Greek modesty, or something else? Either way, it wasn't really any of his business, and he could see nothing to lose by reassuring her.

'But of course,' he said, chivalrously. 'I never doubted it for a second.'

17

True to her word, Selina came back to Martin before noon the following day.

'Have you got something for me?' he asked expectantly.

Selina nodded. 'Could be. Your men are all trained in deep-water reclamation and handling explosives, aren't they?'

'Of course.' It was a plain statement of fact, not a boast.

'Then this could be right up their street,' Selina announced. 'More importantly, it's handy – less than three kilometres off this stretch of coast.'

It sounded promising, Martin thought. 'So what's the actual problem?'

'It's a wreck,' the girl told him. 'One of ours, as it happens. She's lying in about forty metres of water and we have an accurate fix on her position.' She paused, pursing her lips. 'But there are complications.'

'What sort of complications?'

'The sort which make a big bang,' Selina said drily.

Martin sighed. 'Perhaps you'd better give me the

full story. What is this wreck, what was she carrying, and how long has she been down there?'

Selina drew a deep breath. It was obviously going to be a long story, Martin thought. 'She went down in 1966,' Selina began. 'It was a Greek Navy MTB, engaged in laying offshore mines. It was a time when we were still very jumpy about a possible invasion from Turkey. Most of these coastal waters and some of the beaches were mined as a matter of course.'

'What happened to her?' Martin interrupted.

'Nobody's quite sure,' Selina admitted. 'It was nearly twenty years ago remember, and there's not a lot in the records. It's possible that she was attacked with a limpet mine by Turkish frogmen. Another possibility is that there was some sort of an accident. As I said, she wasn't a proper mine-laying vessel, and her crew possibly weren't as properly trained as they might have been. Anyway, she apparently went down very fast, so it's obvious something quite drastic happened to her.'

It was all a very fascinating story, thought Martin, but he couldn't really see where it was leading. 'So what exactly would you like us to do about it?' he asked. 'If she's been on the bottom for this long, the hull will more or less have rusted out by now. You're not imagining there's going to be much worth salvaging, are you?'

Selina shook her head. 'We're quite aware of the probable condition of the wreck,' she said. 'That's just the point. We have no idea how many of her complement of mines she had actually laid before she went down. There could be anything up to a hundred and fifty of the things still left on board. If the hull is starting to break up . . .'

Selina didn't bother to finish the sentence, but Martin got the message clearly enough. Over a hundred mines, nearly twenty years old, corroded and unstable, drifting about loose in the Aegean. It was not a pretty thought. Quite apart from the dangers to commercial shipping, there were a thousand and one other craft to think about. Luxury yachts, speedboats, even jet-skis. Plus, of course, the potential threat to hundreds of pleasure beaches, packed with foreign tourists. The Greek Islands tourist boom was at its height. It would only take one accident to jeopardize the whole future of the industry.

Martin was appalled. He stared at Selina with a shocked, almost accusatory look on his face. 'That's been down there for twenty years and no one's done anything about it before?' He could hardly bring himself to believe the sheer irresponsibility of it.

The girl exhaled noisily and spread her hands in one of those Mediterranean gestures which said nothing but spoke volumes. Martin understood.

'But of course you'd have got round to it sooner or later,' he said acidly.

Selina looked slightly ashamed. 'Well? Can you help us?'

'The actual depth of this wreck – are your people sure that's accurate?'

The girl nodded. 'Absolutely. About forty metres, as I told you.'

'Then we're slightly over the safety margin for scuba gear,' said Martin, as if thinking aloud. 'Anyone working at that depth is going to be strictly limited by decompression time.' He paused, running the standard tables through his head. Three-quarters of an hour working at that depth required a minimum of one full hour of decompression, coming up in three staggered stages. And each diver could safely make no more than two descents in a twenty-four-hour period. Plus, of course, the strict time limitation of the air tanks themselves. He turned his attention back to Selina.

'It would mean a cache of spare air tanks would have to be lowered down on a static line,' he told her. 'And the divers would need to work in pairs so they could help each other change tanks.'

'But it would not be impossible,' Selina prompted.

Martin shook his head. 'No, not impossible. Although for additional safety I'd ideally like to have at least one diver in a regulation suit on hand.' He eyed Selina directly. 'Would your people be willing to make available a boat fitted with a compressor and the right gear?'

'I'm sure that can be arranged,' Selina said without hesitation.

Martin thought for a few more seconds, finally nodding faintly. 'Then we can probably help each other out. I'll have to consult my men, of course. This would necessarily have to be a strictly volunteered operation. I can't order them to do this, you understand?'

'Of course,' Selina agreed, with a faint smile.

'It wouldn't be the English thing to do, would it?'

Martin ignored the gentle jibe. 'So, working on the assumption that we do go ahead, what exactly do you want us to do?'

'A lot is going to depend on the state of the wreck and the number and location of the remaining mines,' Selina said. 'Ideally we'd like everything brought up for safe disposal, but that may not be practical. If the mines are still reasonably packaged together and you consider them safe to handle, then that would be our first choice. But of course any decision would be entirely up to you, and we would accept your professional judgement. On the other hand, if the mines are already loose and scattered, then we would hope you could collect as many as possible.'

'There is another possibility,' Martin pointed out. 'It's quite likely that several of those babies are going to be in an advanced state of corrosion and highly unstable. If they *are* still packed together, that will make for a very dangerous situation indeed.'

'In that case you might have no other choice but to blow the lot,' Selina said. A slight frown crossed her face. Her knowledge of explosives and demolition work was strictly limited. 'I assume that one decent charge would safely detonate them all?'

Martin smiled. 'Oh, you can count on that at least. At that depth, the pressure shock alone would set off anything that's still capable of exploding. It'll make one hell of a big bang, though.'

Selina smiled contentedly. 'Well you did say you wanted something high-profile,' she reminded him.

Every single one of Martin's men volunteered for the dangerous assignment without hesitation. He had never doubted for a second that they would, although he was slightly surprised by how eager most of them seemed to be. They were obviously more bored than he had imagined. A week of inactivity did not sit comfortably with men who had been primed for action and excitement like guns with a hair-trigger.

'So how soon can we get down there?' Sooty asked, beaming. He had already been the first to volunteer for the more uncomfortable job of wearing a regulation diving suit. His obvious enthusiasm provoked the expected wave of sarcasm from his fellows.

'Christ, you're keen, Sooty,' Colin Graham teased him. 'Wouldn't your Mummy let you play with fireworks when you were a kid?'

'I reckon he's just kinky about wearing rubber suits and a brass helmet,' Williams suggested. 'Our Sooty's a closet bondage freak. He'll be standing down there having multiple orgasms while the rest of us are working our balls off.'

Martin cut the banter short. He didn't want the men becoming too hyped up. From what Selina had told him, the job would be far more than some underwater picnic. Far from being a mere diversion, it was likely to be a highly dangerous and volatile assignment, and he didn't want anyone losing sight of the serious dangers involved.

'We'll locate the wreck and make a preliminary recce dive in scuba suits the day after tomorrow,' he announced firmly. 'It will be strictly hands off, observation only, just long enough to determine the state of the hull and the way she's lying. Once we know that, we can start to make more definite plans, and it will give the Greeks time to come up with extra equipment we're going to need.' He looked at Willerbey, who acted as base armourer for the unit. 'I take it we have sufficient stocks of plastic explosive for a job like this, if we do have to rubbish the lot?'

Willerbey grinned at him. 'For a pissing little MTB?' he queried, scornfully. 'Christ, boss, I can break out enough stuff to raise the fucking *Titanic* if we have to.'

Martin smiled thinly. 'That won't be necessary, thank you,' he said. He looked at them all and gave a final nod. 'Well, if that's all settled then I'll let the Greek authorities know we're ready to go ahead.' He left the room, knowing that his men needed the time and freedom to burn off some adrenalin with a bout of joking and general piss-taking. It was always best to leave them to it, and anyway there were a few more details he needed to tie up with Selina now that the project had been unanimously approved.

As Martin left the room, Crewes took the opportunity to pull Willerbey to one side, eyeing him curiously. 'How come you're suddenly looking so bloody chipper again?' he asked. 'You were on a real downer yesterday.'

Willerbey grinned uncomfortably. The odd sense of depression had been lifted away completely now, leaving him feeling slightly embarrassed about the whole episode. 'Maybe I just like blowing things up,' he suggested.

18

With his sceptical attitude towards the Greek way of doing things, Martin had anticipated some difficulties in the actual location of the sunken motor torpedo boat. Efficiency just wasn't a word in the national language, he had more or less decided, so he was pleasantly surprised when the coordinates which Selina had supplied turned out to be remarkably accurate.

The small party of Marines – consisting of himself, Crewes and Willerbey as divers and Williams as pilot of the Rigid Raider – located the wreck within two hours of arriving at the designated spot, using a portable echo-sounder. As Selina had said, she was lying in 140 feet of water, and judging from the sonar trace, still in one piece.

Martin watched Crewes and Willerbey, clad in their black neoprene suits, as they perched somewhat precariously on either side of the craft's sloping, flattened prow. The Raider was not the most suitable boat in the world from which to launch divers, but until the Greeks came up with the properly equipped diving vessel they had promised, it would have to do.

'Now remember that this is just a quick exploration dive,' he reminded them both. 'Once you reach the bottom you'll have only three or four minutes before you start needing decompression time – so the quicker you make it, the faster we can get away again. Just check the position of the wreck, take a couple of photographs and plant a location beacon on the hull. Other than that, you don't touch anything. Is that understood?'

The two divers nodded. 'Put the kettle on, boss,' Crewes said. 'We'll be back in time for tea.'

Martin handed Willerbey the bulky underwater camera, which he clipped to his weight belt. Both divers pulled their masks into position, checked the air flow of their regulators and slipped their breathing tubes into their mouths. With a final thumbs up, each man clapped one hand firmly over the glass front of his mask and tumbled backwards into the water, both jackknifing in unison like a pair of trained seals. With a final flash of black flippers churning up the surface of the water, they were gone.

It felt good to be doing a deep dive again, Crewes thought, as he sliced down through the water with rhythmic, powerful kicks of his legs. Just as Willerbey loved anything which flew, so Crewes felt strangely at home in the water, almost as if it was his natural element. Diving had been his hobby and his passion long before he had joined the SBS, and indeed the knowledge that it would probably make up a substantial part of his service career had been instrumental in his decision to apply in the first place.

The water was unusually clear, even for the Aegean. Crewes supposed that it had something to do with the comparatively narrow channel of water between Samos and the Turkish mainland, which slowed down tidal currents and prevented them from scouring sand and silt up from the seabed. Whatever the reason, the area had traditionally been one of the favourite hunting grounds of the local sponge divers for centuries, and a source of bitter rivalry and feuding between Greeks and Turks both before and after the Cyprus troubles. A few diehards of both nations still managed to scrape a tenuous living diving from their single-masted caiques, although they were already a dying breed. Sheer price had all but killed off the demand for real sponges in the face of opposition from synthetic equivalents, and overfishing by the new types of boat which raked the seabed with huge weighted nets was rapidly depleting those stocks which marine pollution had not yet killed off.

Crewes continued on his way, diving almost vertically into the ever-deepening green of the water. He passed through a tightly packed shoal of small, brightly hued fish, which suddenly burst outwards around him like an exploding firework, throwing out rays of coloured light. He was down to around fifty feet now, and the increased depth had already started to filter out the top end of the spectrum. The water was still clear, but it was taking on a diffused quality which gave the illusion of cloudiness. Directly below him, Crewes saw something grey and bulky undulate across his field of vision and disappear. It could have been a manta ray, but he wasn't sure.

Just over fifteen feet behind him, Willerbey's thoughts were almost the exact opposite of his companion's. Every time he dived, Willerbey was acutely aware that he was out of place, an interloper in a completely alien world. And yet the very strangeness of being in deep water thrilled him in its own unique way. While Crewes revelled in this watery environment, Willerbey felt an ever-present sense of danger which excited him. Feeling the familiar tingle of adrenalin surging through his body, he kicked out with renewed strength, knifing down through the rising column of air bubbles which Crewes left in his wake.

Crewes pulled his left wrist up to his face mask, checking the luminous read-out on his depth gauge. They had reached eighty feet, and were well into a gloomy twilight world where there were no colours other than bottle-green passing into black. Distance itself appeared to be compressed, so that the darkness closed in like an enveloping blanket. It was no longer a time to be diving alone. Crewes stopped kicking for a while, twisting his body in the water to perform a half-turn and look back for Willerbey. He hovered, virtually weightless, until the other man caught up with him. Then, side by side, the two divers continued their descent towards the ocean floor.

The dark bulk of the sunken MTB seemed to materialize suddenly out of the darkness with a faintly shuddering motion, gradually assuming a solid form.

Experienced divers, both men were used to the foreshortening effect of deep water, but the sudden appearance of the wreck came as something of a surprise nevertheless. They stopped kicking, hovering in the water some ten feet above the sunken hulk and turning down the air supply through their regulators. Crewes made a grand gesture of pointing to his watch and holding up three fingers under Willerbey's nose.

Willerbey responded with a thumbs up to show he understood. He unclipped the underwater camera from his belt and dived down again towards the seabed, swimming slowly along the side of the ship towards the prow.

The vessel was tilted only slightly to one side, resting more or less on her belly with her keel buried in the sand. Apart from a luxuriant crop of barnacles and small, razor-edged clams all over the superstructure, she seemed in remarkably good condition, almost undamaged. It was as if some giant hand had simply picked her up from the surface and placed her on the sea bottom, Willerbey thought fancifully. He continued around the prow of the wreck just below deck level, investigating the far side of the hull. It too was intact, as was the entire superstructure. To Willerbey it was a complete mystery why she had gone down. It was not until he had completed his full sweep of the hull and come around the boat's stern that the mystery finally resolved itself.

There *was* no stern! Where the back of the ship should have been there was only a vast, gaping, jagged hole, through which could be seen a crazy abstract sculpture of twisted girders and buckled steel plate before everything was swallowed in a black void. Willerbey brought the camera up to his eyes and backed off until he had the whole scene in frame. For a split second the flash of the camera turned the sunken wreck into a luminous-green ghost ship. Startled by the light, a small octopus flew out of the darkness, jetting towards the diver's face and away over the top of his head. Recovering from a brief moment of shock, he took two more photographs from slightly different angles and glanced at his watch. The three minutes were almost up. It was his last chance to return directly to the surface without making at least two decompression stops on the way up. He looked around for Crewes but there was no sign of him. He had positioned the location beacon and already started back up, Willerbey assumed. Attaching the camera to his belt again, he straightened up in the water and looked upwards, kicking lazily towards the pale-green luminescence of the surface.

A sense of relief filled him as Martin reached over the side of the Rigid Raider to help pull him up and he saw Crewes already wrapping himself in a dry blanket. After scrambling aboard, Willerbey tore off his face mask and spat out his mouthpiece. He began to strip off his tank harness as Williams gunned the twin Johnsons into life and turned the Raider back towards home.

Shivering, Willerbey realized for the first time that he felt chilled through to the bone. Even with a double-skin neoprene wetsuit, the water at 140 feet was wickedly cold, and it didn't take long to leech every drop of heat from the human body. Making a mental note to add an inner thermal layer next time he went down, he accepted a blanket from Martin gratefully, wrapping it tightly around his wet body as the CO produced a large vacuum flask from the floor of the boat and poured the divers a hot coffee. They both sipped it in silence for several minutes.

'Well, what's your assessment of the state of things down there?' Martin asked Willerbey eventually. 'Crewes seems to think that the hull is more or less intact.'

Willerbey described the wreck carefully, in as much detail as he could remember. 'It's certainly going to be no trouble getting in there,' he concluded. 'You could drive a couple of bleeding tanks through that hole in the stern.'

Martin gave a grunt of satisfaction. It made things a lot easier – and a lot safer – if they didn't have to start cutting into the hull or wrenching off rusted hatch covers. 'What do you think happened to her?' he asked after a while.

'She was trying to lay tethered mines, right?' said Willerbey.

Martin nodded. 'That's the information I have.'

Willerbey snorted scornfully. 'Well, that was

sheer bloody stupidity, from an MTB,' he observed. 'And it looks like they paid the price for it. My guess is that the poor dumb bastards managed to suck one of their own mines into the props. Basically, they blew their own fucking arse off. She'll have gone down faster than a whore's drawers on a Saturday night. The crew wouldn't have stood a snowball's chance in hell.'

'Which means there are probably still bodies in there,' Crewes pointed out, with a faint shudder of distaste. 'I suppose the Greeks would like us to recover them as well?'

It was a point Martin hadn't even thought of, and Selina had certainly not mentioned it. He looked at Crewes almost apologetically. 'Yes, I suppose it might be a decent gesture,' he said. 'That's assuming we can bring skeletons up from that depth without them falling to pieces.'

'Damn!' Crewes exploded. 'I hate skeletons. I don't mind blood, or even bodies with bits missing – but skeletons give me the fucking willies.'

With this last morbid observation, he lapsed into silence for the remainder of the journey back to base.

19

It took the Greek authorities a full week to come up with the promised boat and equipment, but Martin wasn't unduly bothered about the delay. He had his cover story now, and with Selina's full cooperation he spent the time setting it firmly in place.

A few telephone calls were made on an open line to order various specialist items of diving equipment, and a few more daylight trips undertaken to the site of the wreck. On Martin's direct orders, his men visited the tavernas of Samos Town and Pythagoria in their off-duty hours and openly discussed the operation so that their conversations might be overheard by the locals. At Selina's instigation, the Greek Coastguard placed clearly visible marker boys in the vicinity of the wreck and issued public shipping warnings that salvage operations would shortly be taking place in the area.

The week was well spent, Martin told himself with satisfaction. By the end of it the perfectly plausible explanation for the presence of British maritime salvage and demolition experts in the area was clear to the most casual observer – let alone anyone who had been making it their business to find out.

And there was a bonus, of course. Underneath all the subterfuge, Bright, Mallory and Janice Reece were quietly getting on with the real work. Inspired by their access to computer design software which was still protected by military secrecy and probably at least two years away from commercial release, they had zipped through the final design stage and were already into the first phase of construction.

Things seemed to be going well, Martin thought, as he prepared to make one of his periodic progress checks around the base. He headed first for the common room, where Pavlaski was conducting a Russian class for some of the men. Besides Selina and himself, only Sergeant Graham spoke Russian fluently, although all the others had at least a working command of the language. It was standard SBS procedure to include lessons in several key languages as part of continuation training, and as long as the Cold War lasted, Russian remained high on the list. Pavlaski's input, however, was twofold. Besides serving as a simple refresher course, his unique knowledge of shipboard slang and the sort of vernacular likely to be used by the average Russian deck-hand might come in useful if the men were verbally challenged. At least, that had been Martin's thinking.

Pavlaski fell silent as Martin entered the room. Martin surveyed his men benignly. 'Everybody having fun?' he asked.

Sooty grinned up at him. 'Great, boss. Next time

I need to tell a Russki that his mother dropped out of a horse's arse, I've got it off pat.'

Martin smiled. 'Keep up the good work, gentle-men,' he said, before turning on his heel and going off in search of Mallory.

The American was putting the finishing touches to a mock-up constructed out of bits of card, balsa-wood, wire and glue. He set it down on his desk as Martin entered. Nodding his head towards the model, he grinned and said: 'Ugly bastard, ain't it?'

Martin had to agree. The machine was indeed an ungainly-looking contraption, lacking the faintest vestige of aesthetic appeal. 'Point is, will it do the job?' he asked.

'Oh, it'll work OK,' Mallory said confidently. 'Just don't expect me to paint my name on the side. This mother could set my business back ten years.' He broke off, seeing that Martin wasn't really in the mood for light-hearted banter. 'Seriously, she's aerodynamically sound, even if she does look like a flying lawnmower. The only detail I haven't finalized yet is the size of the engine – but that's down to you.'

Martin looked puzzled. He didn't understand. 'Why me? I'm no engineer.'

Mallory hastened to explain. 'The engine size is the deciding factor in a complicated set of equations on speed, payload and range. The bigger the engine, the more it weighs and the more fuel it's going to burn. Which means more fuel, more weight – and that comes at the expense of either payload capacity or the distance she'll fly given that amount of fuel.' Seeing the continued bafflement on Martin's face, Mallory picked up a computer printout and handed it to him. 'Look, I've run a whole series of calculations giving you a range of options,' he explained. 'Working on the basis that your average pilot and personal equipment is going to weigh around 85 kilos, you need to tell me which gives you the best deal.'

Martin scanned the sheet of complicated equations and wasn't much wiser. 'Can you simplify this, for a poor layman?' he almost pleaded.

Mallory nodded sympathetically. 'Sure. The sharp end is that it boils down to two key questions. Do you want these birds to fly a short distance fast, a long distance slowly – or do you want the best compromise between the two?'

'And that's it?' Martin asked, slightly surprised that the problem could be expressed that simply.

Mallory let out a short laugh. 'Well, no, not really,' he admitted. 'But you did ask for a simplification.

Martin was thoughtful for a long time, trying to take into account the additional factors which Mallory didn't know about. 'Let's say I was looking for the best of both worlds,' he said after a while. 'What's the best compromise you could offer me?'

Mallory took the computer sheet from Martin and studied it intently. 'OK, I'll narrow it down to two options for you,' he offered. 'You can take a top airspeed of seventy miles per hour and a maximum flying time of two and a half hours. Both dependent on prevailing wind speed and direction, of course. That means your absolute ceiling range is 180 miles, given the best possible conditions.'

Martin considered for a few seconds, shaking his head uncertainly. 'I was hoping for a greater range than that,' he admitted. 'Considerably greater, in fact.'

'OK, let's take a look,' said Mallory. He transcribed one set of equations on to a spare slip of paper and ran a couple of new calculations through a pocket calculator. After scribbling a few lines on the sheet, he looked up at Martin again. 'How about this?' he suggested. 'We use the smallest possible engine that's going to actually keep this beast in the air. That won't be powerful enough to get it off the ground for a static take-off, by the way, so we're going to have to launch from the cliffs straight out over the sea. If one of these babies has to put down for any reason, it'll never get up again.'

'That's perfectly acceptable,' said Martin, sounding more hopeful. 'What does that give us?'

Mallory checked his figures again. 'Top airspeed of around fifty-five miles per hour and enough fuel for four and a half hours of flying time. Say 260 miles – again given optimum weather conditions.'

It was better, but not good enough, Martin thought. 'Any way you can improve on that?' he asked bluntly. 'I need 300 miles.'

Mallory shook his head dubiously. 'Now you're asking for something,' he said. Nevertheless he returned to his calculations and pored over them for several minutes, finally confirming with a faint nod that he had managed to improve the performance figures. 'OK, you've got your 300 miles. It means reverting to the bigger engine and adding another four square metres to the wings, but I'm pretty sure I can do it.'

'Time in the air?' Martin wanted to know. It was the one critical factor he had not discussed with Mallory – mainly for reasons of security. The actual mission depended on making a strike during the hours of darkness. Assuming that the microlights took off from Samos at dusk, that left an absolute maximum of six hours for the attack, including time on the water.

'About four and a half hours. And that's allowing for a standard rate of fuel burn-off, and absolutely no leeway for any kind of safety margin.' Mallory paused as an afterthought struck him. 'Unless . . .'

'Unless what? Is there something else you can do?'

Mallory looked at Martin directly. 'I could probably gain a very small margin for error by modifying the flying harness,' he suggested. 'It really depends on what degree of discomfort your men are prepared to put up with.'

Martin flashed him a wry smile. 'They're not expecting to fly executive class, that's for sure. What are you suggesting?'

'I allowed for a seated harness,' Mallory explained. 'It would give each pilot a more comfortable flying position and a certain degree of flexibility for body movement in the case of cramp or just physical tiredness.'

'And the option?'

'A prone harness. It would be marginally lighter, and it would also cut down wind resistance. The only trouble is, four and a half hours lying stretched out in one fixed position ain't gonna be much fun.'

Martin grinned inwardly. The young American obviously had little idea of the sort of rigours the average SBS Marine went through as part of his day-to-day continuation training. Any man who could hide out for up to five days in a cold and muddy ditch, or survive a week in the wilderness living on whatever food he could find or catch was certainly capable of putting up with a few hours of discomfort.

'Do it,' he said to Mallory. 'They'll cope.'

The faintest trace of admiration showed fleetingly on Mallory's face. 'OK, you got it,' he said. 'It will certainly help.'

Martin felt pleased. Everything seemed to be settled more or less to his satisfaction. 'So when can you get down to construction of the first prototype?' he asked.

'As soon as you dig into that generous back pocket of yours,' Mallory told him flatly. 'Got another handy six or seven grand lying around?'

Martin didn't quibble for a second. 'What do you need?'

'The engines,' Mallory said. 'I'd better have six,

just in case I need to cannibalize one for spares. They don't come cheap.' He picked up a piece of paper from his desk and began to scribble on it. 'There may be other places, but this is the one company in England that I'm confident will have a supply of these spare engines in stock.'

He handed the piece of paper to Martin, who stared at what Mallory had written with a puzzled expression on his face. 'A garden centre in Sussex?'

Mallory nodded. 'British main agents for the American Turfmaster range of industrial grass-cutters,' he explained. 'Best little 150cc engine in the world.' He looked up at Martin, his eyes twinkling with amusement. 'Didn't I tell you this was a flying bloody lawnmower?'

20

The Greeks might have taken their time but they certainly hadn't short-changed him when it came to delivering the goods, Martin conceded. The boat they eventually delivered was a sturdy and serviceable twenty-eight-footer, fully equipped for diving and salvage work with a proper diving platform, main and back-up compressor units, a winch and derrick and even an on-board one-man decompression tank for emergency use. They even offered a crew, which Martin politely declined. Apart from the operating instructions, which were written in Greek, there wasn't a single piece of equipment on board that his men were not completely familiar with and had not been fully trained in the use of.

Martin already had one hundred per cent volunteer status from his men, so there was no problem in picking his final team. The only minor headache was which of the equally enthusiastic Marines he had to disappoint by leaving behind on guard duty at the base. In the end, the task fell to Bailey and Donnelly. With Willerbey and Sooty in regulation diving suits, Crewes and Graham wearing scuba gear and Williams and himself as deck crew, Martin was ready to go.

It was a bright, clear and still morning, with no more than a gentle undulation disturbing the mirror-like surface of the water once they were clear of the coastal swell. Ideal diving conditions, Martin told himself with a sense of satisfaction, and particularly suited to their specific task, should they have to bring up anything especially delicate or volatile.

The journey out to the wreck was as peaceful as a Sunday family boat trip, the only minor excitement being the appearance of a pair of dolphins which they picked up about a mile out, and who frolicked in the bow-waves of the boat for nearly fifteen minutes before finally swimming off at a tangent.

The disappearance of the friendly cetaceans became the starting point for a discussion on sharks and other marine dangers. The four divers spent the rest of the voyage trying to shock and frighten each other with stories of various deep-sea horrors, from Great Whites to stingrays and moray eels. The anecdotes became increasingly horrific and implausible as each man tried to outdo his companions, culminating in Crewes' claim to have known a man who had known a man who had managed to get his sexual equipment bitten clean off by a snapping turtle while swimming naked in a lake in Florida.

It was all harmless fun, Martin reflected, aware that the banter was therapy against the very real perils which a diver could encounter. He remembered his own instructor's words, many years ago: 'A diver without fear is either a liar or a fool.' Equipment and techniques may have improved over the years, but that adage still held true, he felt certain.

Reaching the wreck site, Martin was both surprised and alarmed to find a host of small boats already in the area. Although the one-kilometre exclusion zone marked off by warning buoys was clear, perhaps a dozen fishing vessels and other craft ringed the outer perimeter, bobbing silently at anchor with a quiet air of expectancy. Scanning them quickly, Martin was relieved to see that one of the boats was a small Greek coastguard patrol vessel, obviously there for reasons of safety. So far it hadn't done much of a job, he thought.

'Seems we have company,' Martin muttered unnecessarily.

'Maybe we overdid the public relations bit, boss,' Sooty observed. 'We appear to have attracted a fan club.'

'And not only among the locals,' Crewes pointed out. He jabbed his finger towards a couple of sad double-ended craft anchored hard up against the ring of marker buoys. 'Those are Turkish *trencharidi* – traditional fishing boats. Our fame seems to have spread even further than we anticipated.'

'But what the hell are they doing here?' Martin asked, puzzled and more than a little peeved. He'd wanted the cover operation to get attention, but he had not expected a three-ring circus. And while he could understand a certain amount of morbid curiosity and the presence of a few thrill-seekers, he found that being treated like the high-wire act without a safety net was a little distasteful. They were probably the same sort of people who turned up at the scene of aircraft crashes and other disasters, he reflected bitterly. But that did not explain the presence of the fishing boats.

'Most of them are probably here hoping to see us blow ourselves up,' Willerbey said with a sardonic smile. 'The rest of them are probably just hoping to pick up a few free dinners.'

Martin failed to understand, and the slightly blank expression on his face gave this fact away.

'If we start blasting down there, there's going to be a whole lot of dead fish floating around on the surface,' Willerbey went on to explain. 'Very practical people, the Turks. Waste not, want not – know what I mean?'

Martin understood, finally, although he was still far from happy. 'Well, I want them cleared away,' he growled. He eased the diving boat into the centre of the wreck site and cut the diesel engines. After dropping the anchor, he called over to Williams: 'Get that bloody patrol boat over here and tell the captain I want all these craft moved well clear of the area.'

As it happened, the order was unnecessary, for the patrol boat was already heading in their direction. It took a long time to convince the smiling Greek skipper that the area was dangerous, and even longer for the patrol vessel to drive the circling craft back to what Martin considered to be a safe distance, but they were finally more or less on their own.

'Right, let's all get rigged up,' Martin snapped. 'We've wasted enough time already.' As Crewes and Graham started to pull on their wetsuits, he moved across to help Sooty prepare his own gear.

The two diving suits were brand new, and the only items of equipment Martin had refused to accept from the Greek authorities. It was not a matter of trust, but of personal responsibility. When it came to the safety of his men, Martin found no room for compromise. He had personally supervised the purchase and checking of the two suits and state-of-the-art helmets, and the hefty bill he had forwarded home reflected their quality.

He helped Sooty clamber into the bulky, cumbersome and extremely heavy suit. It was a slow and laborious task, but then regulation suits had never been designed for speed and efficiency. Essentially a thick layer of rubber bonded between two other layers of heavy twill fabric, a diving suit needed to be as robust as the job demanded. And when working under pressure which could crush a man's ribcage like papier mâché, or squeeze brain tissue out through his nasal cavities, those demands were pretty heavy.

With Sooty finally suited up, Martin lifted the heavy copper and brass helmet and placed it gingerly over the man's head, screwing it firmly down into the heavy-duty metal seating ring built into the neck of the suit. He unbolted and opened the hinged face-plate before coupling up the air hose and safety lines. It was time for a final safety check. Martin waved over to Williams, waiting by the compressor. 'Start her up for a test run,' he called out.

The compressor engine fired into life with a brief roar, quickly settling down to a quiet, regular throbbing. Martin turned back to Sooty. 'Ready for final test?'

'Ready when you are,' the man replied. He closed his face-plate, screwing the retaining wing-nuts finger-tight. It would be down to Martin to complete full pressurization checks when the time came for descent, but for now the helmet's highly efficient seals were good enough for a test at normal atmospheric pressure.

Martin gave the man a full three minutes before tapping lightly on the glass front of the face-plate. 'Everything all right?' he mouthed, exaggerating his lip movements.

Sooty raised one gloved hand in a thumbs-up gesture. It was easier than trying to nod with the cumbersome helmet on his head. Martin unscrewed the face-plate again, waving over at Williams to cut the compressor. 'All right, everything appears to check out,' Martin said. 'Let's run through procedures, shall we? I'm sending you down five minutes ahead of the others. We'll be using your safety line as a tethering point for their spare tanks, so make sure you're in their field of vision at all times.'

'Got it, boss,' Sooty replied, realizing the importance of the CO's order. When the time came for the two scuba divers to start their two-stage ascent to the surface, they would already be running short of air. They would need fresh tanks fast, and they would need to find them easily. Sooty himself would be their beacon, and his hose and safety line a direct route to follow.

'You'll send whatever bodies you can find up first,' Martin went on. 'You'll take a net down with you when you go. It'll be on a separate line to the winch, so make sure you don't get it fouled up with your own lines. By the time that job's done, Crewes and Graham will be ready to start coming up, so you're going to be down there on your own for about fifteen minutes while they make their first stop at thirty-five feet. Just relax and enjoy the scenery, and don't try to be a hero. Got it?'

'Your word is my command, boss,' replied Sooty. There was a grin on his face as he spoke, but his voice was in deadly earnest. At a hundred feet, without backup divers, a man went by the book and did exactly what he was told.

'OK, then we're ready to go,' Martin said. At his signal, Williams started up the compressor again. Martin closed Sooty's face-plate for the last time, and carefully tightened the retaining bolts. After a final check of the helmet's hose couplings, he rapped briefly on the glowing brass dome and stepped back as the man's suit pressurized and took on the appearance of a slightly anorexic sumo wrestler.

With a final grin through the face-plate, Sooty

began to trudge awkwardly towards the edge of the diving platform in his heavy weighted boots. He waited patiently as Williams hooked him up to the launch harness then swung him out over the surface of the water. There was time for one last thumbs up before Williams returned to the winch and Sooty began to drop slowly into the waiting sea.

Martin watched until the burnished brass top of his helmet had disappeared below the surface of the water before turning back to Crewes and Graham to give them their final orders.

21

It was a long time since he'd dived in a full regulation suit, and the restricted visibility hit him with something of a shock. Twenty feet down, Sooty felt a moment of near panic as the claustrophobia closed in on him. He was surrounded by a total and suffocating darkness, with only blurred tunnel vision of greenish light directly ahead of him. Above the faint hissing of air inside his helmet, he could hear only the steady thud of his own heartbeat.

He remembered, then, that he could move his head from side to side. The feeling of panic began to subside as he swung the heavy helmet in a wide arc, taking in more of his surroundings and adding breadth and perspective to his vision. He relaxed, enjoying the sensation of near weightlessness and the patterns of light refracting down through the smoky-green water as the winch lowered him slowly towards the seabed.

His heavy leaded boots made contact with the sandy bottom before he quite expected it. Another brief moment of shock rippled through him – a strange, detached sense of wonder which was only just this side of fear. Perhaps it was something that no diver ever got fully used to, Sooty reflected. This sudden knowledge that he was somewhere he just didn't belong, a trespasser in a world which was so utterly alien it seemed almost like a living force, duty-bound to find some way in which to eject or destroy him.

Again he fought against the strange fantasy by taking his bearings, establishing a point of reference. He shuffled himself around until he was directly facing the shadowy bulk of the sunken MTB. They had dropped him well clear of any possible obstructions – perhaps twenty or thirty feet from the stern. He assumed that, guided by the signal from the location beacon, Williams must know his exact position, and would have already paid out enough slack on his safety line to allow him the appropriate range of movement. It was something to check, anyway, before he set out towards the wreck. After dropping the weighted retrieval net on the seabed beside his feet, he shuffled a few steps sideways and then flexed his knees, making a couple of practice jumps to test that his lines were free and unobstructed. His body rose and fell in the water in cartoon-like slow motion, like some surrealistic mime artist. A vision of astronaut Buzz Aldrin bounding across the surface of the moon swam into his mind, making him smile. He stooped down to pick up the retrieval net again. 'One small step for man,' he murmured to himself, parodying Neil Armstrong's historic utterance as he began to move ponderously towards the stern of the wreck.

*   *   *

'OK, he's on the bottom and moving,' Williams said, paying out a few more yards of air hose and safety line over the edge of the diving platform.

It was the cue for Crewes and Graham to waddle over to join him. 'You look like a pair of plastic ducks,' Williams told them, grinning all over his face. The two scuba divers had exchanged their usual black suits for bright-yellow ones, their normal concern with camouflage having been replaced by the need for high visibility.

'Quack bloody quack,' Crewes shot back. The two divers paused at the edge of the platform, synchronizing their watches and checking their air regulators.

Martin had walked over to join them. 'OK, you know what to do,' he told them. 'Just follow Sooty's air hose all the way, and don't forget to check the depth of those spare tanks as you go down.' There was one last point Martin felt worth mentioning, given the circumstances. The men's need, sometimes, to negate the horror and finality of death with a little black humour could sometimes result in the odd prank of dubious taste. 'And try to show a bit of respect for any bodies,' he muttered darkly. 'The Greeks are watching us, so no sick practical jokes, please.'

He regretted saying it almost as the words left his mouth, as both men regarded him with hurt, even censorious expressions on their faces. It was too sombre a note on which to send them down, he realized. Forcing a grin on to his face, he tried to lighten the situation. 'Oh, and bring me back a couple of decent-sized lobsters, if you can find any.'

The ploy worked. The men brightened perceptibly. 'Settle for an octopus, boss?' Crewes asked. 'We could all have calamary for tea.'

Williams interrupted the banter, after an anxious glance at his watch. A stickler for routine, he was concerned about the precise timings he had already worked out. Sooty had now been on the bottom for eight minutes.

'Time to go, you pair of clowns,' he bellowed. 'You're late for your date.'

Crewes and Graham pulled their masks into place, approaching the edge of the diving platform. They jumped in together feet first, jackknifed in the water and began to dive, following the line of Sooty's air hose.

Sooty stood in the mouth of the gaping hole in the stern of the torpedo boat, waiting for his companions to join him before venturing any further. The blast which had sent the stricken vessel to the bottom had left great jagged sheets of buckled and twisted plating in the metal hull. Although they now appeared to be softened and rounded, being deceptively covered in marine growth, Sooty was in no doubt that they could still slice through an air hose like razors. Until Crewes and Graham turned up to help guide him into the MTB's gloomy interior, he was taking no chances.

Bored with waiting, and almost hypnotized by the faint and regular throb of the compressor motor transmitting down his hose and lines, he was blissfully unaware of the two divers as they cut down almost vertically through the water towards him.

It was so obvious that he had not heard or sensed their descent, Graham realized, as he neared the motionless diver. The opportunity to give the unfortunate man a shock almost screamed out at him, and he was unable to resist it. He detached his heavy underwater torch from his belt as he hovered in the water directly above Sooty's head. Then, with a sideways glance and a wink at Crewes, he reached down and rapped the torch twice against the back of Sooty's helmet.

It is not easy to make a man wearing lead-weighted boots jump, but Graham managed it. Every nerve in Sooty's body tensed as the sound of the torch blows reverberated inside his metal helmet like the knell of doom. Involuntarily, his muscles responded with a reflex action as adrenalin flooded into his system, triggering the 'fight or flight' response. Arms flailing sluggishly in the water, he cleared the bottom by a good eight inches and threw himself forward, trying desperately to break into a run. Kicking out with his flippers, Graham propelled himself forward, cleaving through the water past the panicking diver to hover directly in his path.

Sooty checked himself as the yellow flash in his peripheral vision resolved into a recognizable image. His heart pounding, he tried to let his body go limp, glaring out through the face-plate towards the wickedly grinning face behind the mask.

'Bastard,' he mouthed through the glass. He shivered briefly as his fear dissipated, then broke into a nervous, trembling fit of the giggles.

Crewes swam down to join them. He made a gesture of pointing to his watch, then signalled forty-five minutes by opening and closing his fist. It was a reminder that their working span was strictly limited, and it was time to get to serious business. Sooty nodded, the task being easier in water, and pointed towards the dark interior of the MTB before raising his hand above his head and indicating his breathing hose.

The two scuba divers understood the message. Taking up a position either side and slightly in front of him, a few feet above the top of his helmet, they led him slowly into the gaping black maw of the breached stern, placing their bodies protectively between his air hose and the top of the hole.

From outside, the interior of the ship had merely looked gloomy and forbidding. Six feet in, and it was almost pitch-blackness, broken only by a few foggy patches of dull and greenish luminescence where some residual light from the sea above crept in through patches of corrosion in the overhead deck.

Crewes and Graham snapped on their torches, probing the depths of the cavernous hull with the bright beams. Like the house lights suddenly going up in a darkened theatre, the interior of the vessel was abruptly the stage-set of some grisly tableau.

Despite the softening effect of marine growths and heavy encrustations of barnacles and shellfish, the scene of utter devastation was still obvious. Shattered and twisted girders criss-crossed the interior of the hull at crazy angles, some propped up against each other so precariously that it looked as though a mere ripple in the water would cause them to fall.

The first skeleton was just inside the hole, lying against the down-tilted side of the ship. It looked as though it had been thrown there by some giant and careless hand. The poor bastard had probably caught the full blast of the explosion, Crewes thought with a shudder. The skull, spine and ribcage appeared more or less intact, although there was only one arm. The other arm, and both legs, were missing.

Graham located another body at the far end of the hull, its skeletal arms still wrapped around the wheel of the inner hatchway door, which had remained intact. The unfortunate sailor had obviously been crushed there by the pressure of the inrushing water before he'd had a chance to turn the wheel. Incongruously, the man's synthetic deck shoes were still on his bony feet.

The first priority was to move him, Graham realized. If the hatchway could still be opened, it would afford comparatively easy access to the other areas below deck level. Stores and ammunition caches would have been kept in the fore section of the boat, so if there were any remaining mines, that was where they would be. He swam over to Crewes, directing his attention to the area and communicating his suggestions by hand signals.

Crewes understood. Together the two scuba divers made their way back to the skeleton, taking it up gently between them and transporting it back out to the open sea, where they lay it gingerly in the retrieval net. Martin's last warning rang in Graham's ears. It seemed a trifle undignified to load the shattered bones of the second corpse in as well. There was always the chance that they could yet come across the missing limbs, although it was more likely that they had been dragged away by scavengers at the time, when there was still meat on the bones.

After signalling for the net to be lifted by a couple of tugs on the main rope, they returned inside the hull to try and open the hatchway.

Surprisingly the hatch wheel was still free enough to be moved by hand, even after nearly two decades. The door itself, however, was not. Despite repeated tugs by both divers, it refused to budge.

There were two possibilities, Crewes figured. The door might simply be rusted in place, or it was warped – either from the initial blast of the explosion or from the impact of the wreck hitting the bottom. He placed his face-mask close to his colleague's with an unspoken question in his eyes. Tapping his belt, he indicating the small amount of plastic explosive and fuses he had brought down with him in case of emergency.

Graham shook his head, his expression dubious. They had no way of knowing what was on the other side of the hatch, or how close it was lying to the door frame. An explosion – even a small one –

was probably not a very good idea while there was anyone still in the water, and he was aware that Crewes carried only three-minute fuses. If the hatch had to be blown at all, then it would have to be done from the surface, by remote detonation. Short of using up the best part of another full day in placing the charge, decompressing and clearing the surface area, there remained only the option of trying brute force.

He dived to the floor of the sunken hull, scanning the various pieces of debris and wreckage with his torch for a suitable blunt instrument. A piece of broken metal spar about eighteen inches long looked ideal. Graham carried it back to the hatchway and jammed it behind the side of the wedged door. Getting sufficient leverage while free-floating in water was no easy matter, but with Crewes' help and a great deal of effort, the door finally sprang open.

With a gentle kick of his flippers, Graham propelled himself through the hatch. As he had suspected, he was in the munitions storage area of the boat. Sweeping the area with his torch, he could see that damage was minimal here, although much of what would have been neatly stacked equipment had been strewn around the floor as the vessel settled on the bottom.

There was another corpse. It was undamaged, and still had shreds of rotting and tattered uniform clinging to the bones. A faint glint of metal reflected back the light of the torch as Graham swept the beam over it, and he moved in for a closer inspection.

The skeletal fingers were tightly clenched around something small and silvery. Curious, Graham reached down to inspect the object in greater detail. It was a small silver locket on a chain, its hinged face wide open. The photograph that it must have once contained was now dissolved away, but Graham had no doubts that the unfortunate seaman must have spent his final moments taking a last fond look at his wife or sweetheart, even as the waters rose to drown him.

Graham backed away from the skeleton, hovering in the water well clear of the floor and took another good look around the area. Unless there was anything else up on deck, it looked as though the vessel had more or less completed its task when the accident occurred, he decided. There were no mines to be seen, although there were perhaps a dozen unopened crates strewn around the floor which might merit further investigation. On balance, however, Graham considered it unlikely that the vessel still contained anything more explosive than shells for the pair of 40mm guns mounted fore and aft on deck, and they would now be virtually harmless. As the mine-laying mission had taken place in what was ostensibly peacetime, it was unlikely that the boat had been carrying any live torpedoes. All in all, it would seem that the sunken MTB posed no threat at all, considering the depth she was lying in. If the Greeks didn't consider her worth salvaging, there seemed no reason why she should not be left where she was, to rust away. If nothing else, it gave the fish something interesting to look at, he thought wryly – like an ornamental stone at the bottom of the aquarium.

He flipped himself back through the hatch to summon Crewes. They'd get this body out and then conduct a search of the upper superstructure, he thought. The ship would have normally carried a complement of eighteen men, and yet so far they had found only three bodies. Unless there were any more trapped on the bridge or in the radio room, most of the crew on deck at the time of the disaster must have been pulled down in the plummeting vessel's suction wave and dispersed to their individual fates.

Crewes nudged Graham gently, jabbing his finger at his watch as the retrieval net began to rise towards the surface, carrying the last of the seven bodies they had been able to find. Their diving time had expired; it was time to make their way up to their first decompression point at forty-five feet. The two scuba divers swam over to Sooty, who was using the rest of his time to search through the wreckage in a vain attempt to find the missing bones of the first skeleton. Communicating their intention to return to the surface, they handed him one of the torches, waved their farewells and left him to his self-imposed task.

A sense of great loneliness descended on Sooty as the two brightly coloured divers passed out of his field of vision. Even though there had been no communication other than by hand signals, their physical presence alone had given him a sense of comradeship and comfort. Now, with their departure, he was suddenly and acutely aware of that strange feeling of alienation again.

Lieutenant-Colonel Martin's last words rang in his ears. 'Just relax and enjoy the scenery, and don't try to be a hero.'

At the time, it had seemed like good advice — as it was now. Sooty turned slowly towards the gaping hole in the stern, picking his way carefully over the twisted wreckage beneath his feet. He would get himself clear of the wreck and wait in open water until they were ready to start pulling him up for his own decompression sequence.

He stepped on the raised corner of a buckled deck plate, which moved slightly under his weight, dislodging two or three other pieces of debris which had been resting against it. The sudden and unexpected movement made Sooty look down in alarm, sweeping the floor of the wreck with his torch for anything else which might be loose and potentially dangerous.

Something white gleamed underneath the dislodged wreckage. Sooty bent down, grasping the upturned edge of the buckled plate with his gloved hands and trying to pull it sideways. It refused to budge. Shifting his footing, he moved to the other side, attempting to tear the plate loose from a different angle. It began to bend slightly, as though it was about to come free, then jammed again. Perhaps it would come free if he tried to pull it upwards, he thought. Changing his grip, and taking a firm hold, he gave the plate a sharp, vertical tug.

There was a moment of resistance, and then the single half-rusted bolt which had been keeping the plate in place gave way under the strain. The plate snapped away abruptly, coming free in Sooty's hands. Its unexpected release caught him unawares and off balance. He toppled backwards, the rear of his helmet making contact with something very hard and metallic which sent a wave of noise and vibration rattling through his brain. Slightly dazed, he was only dimly aware of his back crashing against an upright girder which lurched sideways with a shriek of tortured metal. Then it was beginning to topple away and Sooty was falling on to his back in slow motion, gazing up through his face-plate in horrified fascination as a pair of cross-members plummeted towards his head.

'Oh shit!' Williams screamed out at the top of his voice, commanding Martin's and Willerbey's concerned attention immediately. The shocked look on Williams' face alone was enough to tell them both that his outburst was far more than a curse of mere annoyance.

Martin jumped across the deck towards him. 'What the hell is it?' he demanded.

Williams was trembling with shock. 'I just got three fours on the safety line,' he said, his voice breaking slightly. 'And Graham and Crewes will already be on their way up. Sooty's down there on his own – and he's in trouble.'

The information seeped into Martin's brain like

an ice-cold draught, fanning it into mental over-drive. Four tugs on a safety line, repeated three times, was a clear, internationally recognized signal that a diver was in danger. It would only be used in a matter of extreme urgency.

'What about the pressure? Is he getting his air?' Martin snapped, voicing the first thought which came into his head.

Williams glanced at the pressure gauges on the compressor. 'She's reading normal,' he confirmed quickly. 'There's no sign of any problem with the air hose or the suit.'

'Then he's either injured or trapped by an obstruc-tion. Maybe both,' Martin said, running through the next most likely possibilities. 'Try to bring him up – very slowly.'

Williams started the winch, easing it into low gear very gently. It ran smoothly for several seconds, tak-ing up the slack in the diver's hose and safety lines. Then, as the lines went taut, the winch's automatic safety clutch detected resistance and jumped into neutral, with the grating sound of slipping gears.

'Shit,' Williams yelled again. 'What the hell do we do now?'

Willerbey was already stripping off his clothes. 'I'm going down,' he announced, crossing the deck and strapping one of the spare sets of air tanks across his naked back. 'Crewes and Graham won't be up for another thirty-five minutes, and they'd need at least another hour before they could make a second dive.'

Martin grabbed the man's arm, restraining him.

'There may not be anything you can do,' he warned Willerbey. 'And if you get trapped down there by the need to decompress, we'll have blown every chance we have.'

Willerbey shook his head, disengaging himself from Martin's grip. 'I'm not going to be down there long enough,' he said. 'I'll pull myself straight down Sooty's air hose, check the position and head straight back up again. Two minutes, maximum.'

The man was not going to listen to any objections, Martin realized, so he didn't try. Under similar circumstances, he knew that he would do the same thing himself. He stood back as Willerbey pulled on a pair of flippers and grabbed a spare face-mask. Otherwise completely naked, he ran across to the edge of the diving platform and threw himself into the sea.

Willerbey cleaved down through the water, pulling himself hand over hand straight down Sooty's air hose while kicking out frantically at the same time. He reached Crewes and Graham, hovering at forty-five feet, in seconds. Pausing only for frantic signals for them to continue decompressing as normal, he flashed past them again, leaving the two divers exchanging puzzled and worried looks.

At a hundred feet the coldness of the water cut into his body like a knife, filling him with a very real fear that he would get cramp and not be able to carry on. He forced himself to think of lying out on a beach on a blazing hot summer's day and continued to pull himself towards the hull of the wreck, which was now visible as a great black and shapeless blur. Then he was at the stern of the vessel itself, following Sooty's air hose into the interior of the wreck and noting that it was wedged tightly into the top of a jagged V of torn metal. It was a good thing that the safety cut-out on the winch was so sensitive, he thought. A couple of pounds more pull and the hose would have been severed like a pruned sapling.

He pushed himself through the hole and located Sooty. The diver was lying on his back but apparently uninjured. Willerbey peered into the face-plate of the diving helmet to check if the man was conscious. Sooty looked frightened, but he managed a weak, almost apologetic smile.

There was nothing lying across his body, Willerbey noted at once. He was held down only by a couple of heavy spars which had glanced off the dome of the helmet, entangled themselves in the hose and lines, and dragged him down to his present position. The lines were still pinned securely to the floor, and one glance was enough to tell Willerbey that they were too heavy to lift away on his own. There was nothing he could do immediately, and no time to stop there to think about it. He tapped Sooty's helmet briefly in what was intended to be a gesture of reassurance, then kicked himself clear of the wreck and struck out for the surface.

Both Martin and Williams were leaning over the side of the diving platform expectantly as he broke the surface and hauled himself up over the edge, spitting out his mouthpiece and snorting. There was liquid in his mask. For a moment, Willerbey thought it was leaking, but then he lifted the mask clear of his face and saw that the liquid was blood, and it was coming from his nose.

Ignoring it, he delivered a succinct appraisal of the situation, which Martin considered hastily.

'How long can he last out?' he demanded. 'I mean, will his air hose hold good until we can get Crewes and Graham back down there to free him?'

Willerbey shrugged. 'Your guess is as good as mine, boss. Air's still getting through at the moment, but the stuff lying across the hose is pretty heavy and it could settle down even more. Besides, it looked as though there's some other loose junk which could come down on him at any moment. We may not have enough time to wait for Crewes and Graham.'

Martin looked grim. 'I don't see that we have much choice,' he said grimly.

'There is one chance,' Williams put in quietly, although there was a great deal of doubt in his voice.

Martin and Willerbey looked up at him hopefully, eager to seize upon the slightest note of optimism.

'Sooty's gear is about the best you can get,' Williams said flatly. 'That helmet he's wearing is fitted with a highly sophisticated safety check valve on the air intake. If the air supply is cut off for any reason, it seals itself off automatically, leaving the diver with whatever air is left in the helmet and the rest of the suit. Even at that depth, it would probably give him three to four minutes before it fouled up.'

'So what are you suggesting?' Martin asked.

'That we get a spare safety line down to him, slice through his air hose and lines, and pull him straight up,' Williams said.

Martin shook his head vehemently as he said: 'He's been down there for over fifty minutes, for Christ's sake. Bringing him straight up from that depth would kill him. His blood would be bubbling like a damn steam geyser.'

'We've got the on-board decompression tank,' Williams reminded him. 'If we got him out of his suit and straight into that, he should have a reasonable chance of survival.'

'Odds?' Willerbey asked.

Williams shrugged. 'Say sixty-forty on the plus side?' he suggested, with brutal honesty.

Willerbey thought about it, trying to place himself in Sooty's position as a fellow diver. Given the same odds, he'd probably go for it,' he reflected. Especially when the only other choice was lying there helplessly with every second seeming like an hour, just waiting to be crushed or suffocated at any moment.

The other side of the coin, of course, was the sheer physical hell that Sooty would have to go through. As Martin had already pointed out, bringing a pressurized diver straight up from 140 feet would place an almost unendurable strain on his body. Willerbey had suffered a case of the bends himself once, after making an emergency ascent because of a faulty regulator. But that had been from only forty-five feet and after thirty minutes underwater.

The intolerable pain of that experience would be only a pale shadow of the agony which Sooty would undoubtably suffer before they managed to get him into the decompression tank.

On balance, though, Willerbey felt sure that it would be Sooty's choice, if he were given the option. He made a decision on the man's behalf. 'Then let's do it,' he blurted out.

Martin looked at him sternly. 'You know I can't let you go down again,' he said heavily. 'Two crash-dives in a row and you're likely to pop both your eardrums, or even worse.'

But Williams had already darted over to the supply locker to break out a fresh coil of nylon rope and connect it up to the winch, and Willerbey was pulling his mask back into place. He looked up at Martin, grinning recklessly. 'I think I must have done that already, boss. I can't hear a fucking word you're saying.'

Martin was powerless to stop him as he snatched the free end of the rope from Williams' hands and jumped over the side again. He went down more slowly this time, knowing that a few more seconds were unlikely to make much difference. Once he had Sooty cut free and on his way up, he had a good forty-five minutes of air in his tanks. He could afford to take his time coming up again, decompressing as normal. Closer to the surface, the water would be considerably warmer.

He reached the stricken diver and realized that he had been right in his choice. Sooty must have moved his body slightly, disturbing the debris beneath him and allowing some of the heavier stuff above to settle down even more. The bulky cross-member had sunk down only a few inches, but it was already showing signs of kinking the pressurized air hose. The slightest degree of further movement and it would be starting to crush the hose, cutting back Sooty's air supply and possibly triggering off the automatic shut-down valve in his helmet.

Hovering above the man in the water, Willerbey reached down and pulled the heavy diver's knife from Sooty's belt. Watching his face carefully, he mimed out his proposed plan of action so that the man would have a rough idea of what was going on.

A brief flicker of anguish showed in Sooty's eyes as he interpreted Willerbey's gestures. An experienced diver, he was fully aware of the score. It would have taken a superhuman to face the harsh realities of the situation without showing some emotion. Finally, his expression softening to one of resignation, he nodded faintly, giving Willerbey his approval.

Gingerly, Willerbey pulled in the slack on the nylon rope until it was nearly taut, then looped it under the diver's armpits into a makeshift harness and secured it firmly. Then, taking the razor-sharp knife, he slashed first through the old safety line and finally, after a momentary pause, through the air hose. The water around Sooty's head seemed to froth and boil, suddenly, as the pressurized air gushed out in huge glittering bubbles. Giving a double tug on the rope, Willerbey guided the helpless diver through the water towards the hole in the stern as Williams started the winch to pull him back up to the surface.

Clearing the wreck, Willerbey followed him up for about sixty feet and then paused, treading water. He'd give himself a good fifteen minutes to decompress, he told himself. There was nothing else he could do for Sooty now, and his fate was firmly in the more than capable hands of Williams and Lieutenant-Colonel Martin. Looking up, as the diver continued to rise steadily towards the surface, Willerbey couldn't help wondering if he had saved the man's life, or merely sent him to a different, and more excruciating death.

Sooty was alive but in bad shape as Williams winched him up over the side of the diving platform and lowered him gently to the deck. Contorted in agony, he lay there helplessly with his body twitching and convulsing obscenely as fresh waves of pain tore through him.

Martin rushed to kneel at the man's side, hastily unbolting the heavy helmet and pulling it clear from his head. A froth of blood and saliva bubbled from between Sooty's compressed lips, and his eyes were rolling wildly, like a madman's. God only knew the pain he was suffering, Martin thought, bitterly regretting the fact that he could do nothing to ease it. Although there were painkillers and sedatives in the ship's medical kit, he could not use them. Once in the decompression tank, Sooty would need the full reserves of his strength and bodily systems operating at peak efficiency if he was to survive.

Williams had already prepared the decompression unit. Leaving the winch, he hurried over to help Martin get the diver out of his suit. Together they managed to lift the screaming, thrashing man across the deck and into the coffin-sized tank. Closing and bolting the heavy lid, Williams switched on the compressor to pressurize it and stood back, glancing at Martin with a question in his eyes.

It was a question Martin couldn't answer. The two men stood watching the tank helplessly as the unit pumped itself up to the pre-set pressure and cut off automatically.

'He needs to get to a proper unit fast,' Williams pointed out. 'And we've got another twenty-five minutes to wait for the other divers. Think the Greeks would help out?'

'Damn right they will,' Martin said firmly. He headed for the ship's radio, to summon the Greek patrol boat which was still waiting outside the ring of marker buoys. Moments later the vessel was lying alongside the diving boat.

Martin's Greek wasn't good, but he considered it adequate to convey the nature of the emergency. In the event it wasn't necessary as the Greek captain spoke near-perfect English and was more than willing to help.

'What can I do for you?' he asked politely.

Martin didn't bandy words. 'Where's the nearest full decompression unit with hospital facilities?' he asked.

The Greek looked slightly apologetic. 'There's nothing on Samos or the neighbouring islands, I'm afraid. The nearest would be in Piraeus, on the mainland.'

'Could you get our man there?' Martin asked. 'We can detach the tank and winch it over to you.'

The captain nodded. 'Of course. I can call for a helicopter to meet us halfway. It will save time.'

'Thanks,' Martin said warmly, relief surging through him. He glanced at Williams, but didn't need to say anything. The man was already moving towards the winch to prepare a carrying cradle for the portable compression tank. Once pressurized, it could be simply unbolted from the deck and would maintain its pressure indefinitely.

The whole operation took less than three minutes. With the tank safely stowed on deck, the Greek patrol boat moved slowly back out through the ring of marker buoys and the few ships which remained in the area before throttling up and disappearing towards the mainland at full speed.

22

Sooty was going to make it. It had taken the Greek medics two days to stabilize him and a further week to rule out the possibility of permanent internal organ or brain damage, but they had finally given him the all clear.

That was Lieutenant-Colonel Martin's good news. The downside was that the man was going to need at least four weeks to recuperate, which effectively scrubbed him from the mission. It was a setback which Martin could have done without. Along with Sergeant Graham, Williams, Crewes and Willerbey, Sooty had always been on the priority list to take part in the actual raid, and now Martin was down to his two reserves of Bailey and Donnelly. Although both men were seasoned and reliable Marines, they lacked the degree of microlight experience shared by the others.

Other than that, things appeared to be going reasonably well, Martin felt. Diving on the sunken MTB was now finished, and the civilian conscripts had made the most of their time. Bright had already put three hulls in the water and had finished off all his flotation tests to his satisfaction. He had managed to fit temporary booms and rigs to two of them so that Randy Havilland could begin his windsurfing courses for the men. Mallory was well advanced on the basic frame for the prototype microlight and the engines had arrived from England. However, it seemed that the American had something on his mind.

'What's the problem?' Martin asked, after going to his room in response to the man's request.

'Not really a problem,' Mallory said. 'More like a little mystery, really. I think someone's been accessing my computer designs.'

The American might not consider it of much importance, but Martin most certainly did. His eyes narrowed. 'Are you sure?'

Mallory shrugged again. 'Well, I think so.'

'Think – or know? What grounds do you have for suspicion?'

Mallory crossed the room to the printer connected up to the computer. 'Come over here,' he invited Martin, waiting until the man joined him to point to the print-run indicator. 'See that?'

Martin looked. The figure was 004. 'So?' he asked.

'So there's an extra print I can't account for. I made three in all – one for Bright, one for Janice and one for myself. That was over a week ago, and I haven't used the printer since.'

'Could either of the others have run off an extra copy without telling you?'

Mallory nodded. 'Sure, they *could* have, but they didn't. I've asked them both.'

'And you're sure the counter was set at zero when you first used it?'

Mallory looked slightly unsure of himself. 'No, to be honest; that's the one thing I'm not one hundred per cent sure of,' he admitted. 'It wasn't something I thought of checking at the time.' He paused, eyeing Martin querulously. 'But it was a brand-new unit, wasn't it? All of this stuff was straight out of the packing cases, as far as I know.'

Martin nodded faintly, looking worried. He'd personally supervised the unpacking and setting-up of the equipment. To his knowledge, no one had even switched on the system until Mallory had used it. 'What about quality-control checks?' he asked, grasping at straws. 'Don't manufacturers run a working test on equipment before they ship it out?'

Again, Mallory looked unsure. 'I guess they might,' he said. 'But then if they're going to be that finicky, why not reset the counter back to zero at the same time, just for the sake of appearances?'

Martin didn't attempt an answer. He was too busy worrying the matter over in his mind. As Mallory had said, it was a mystery rather than a problem, and an inconclusive one at that. But a mystery nevertheless. Another one!

'Damn,' Martin growled, slamming his clenched fist down on Mallory's worktop. He took a deep breath, recovering himself. 'If there was another copy run off, when was it done, do you think?'

Mallory shook his head. 'Could have been any time in the last week. Like I said, I haven't used the printer since then. I only noticed it a few minutes ago, quite by accident.'

'All right, I'll check around and see if there's anything I can find out,' Martin said rather helplessly. 'Just keep your eyes open and let me know if anything else unusual happens.' There wasn't much else he could do. Feeling totally impotent, he left the room.

He found Selina in the common room by accident rather than design. Though she had been his first thought for the most likely suspect, Martin had not intended to tackle her directly, feeling that there would be little point. She would of course simply deny any direct accusation, and it would not be a good idea to antagonize her while he still needed her trust and cooperation. Now, however, the opportunity presented itself to at least sound her out, using a little discretion. He forced a cheery smile.

'Time off on your own?' he said chattily. 'I thought you might be with young Havilland. You two seem to get on well together.'

The girl flashed him a guarded smile. Martin wasn't usually the chatty type, and it immediately put her on the alert. Her eyes held a faintly mocking challenge.

'Are we doing a little prying? Trying to find out if Randy and I have got something going?'

Faced with such a frank question, Martin shook his head, feeling embarrassed. 'No, not at all,' he protested.

Selina seemed unconvinced. 'Or perhaps you

were wondering if I'd been pumping him for information on this little project of yours,' she went on. 'In which case the answer is most definitely no, and you can ask Randy for confirmation.'

The conversation was definitely not going the way he had intended, Martin thought. 'I don't think that will be necessary,' he muttered, trying to lighten things up again.

'Perhaps it might be very necessary,' Selina said, with a curious little undertone in her voice. She paused, staring hard at him. 'Look, you're suspicious of me, and I can understand that.'

The woman's uncanny ability to penetrate matters on an instinctive level rattled Martin again. It was almost as if she could read his mind. With some effort he met her gaze. 'What makes you think that?' he asked warily.

Selina looked vaguely irritated. 'Because it is in the very nature of our jobs to be suspicious of other people. And because I think you fail to understand one of the fundamental subtleties of the Greek mentality,' she told him.

'Which is?'

Selina allowed herself a faint smile. 'For want of a better expression let's call it a sense of detachment,' she said. 'Does it not occur to you that we might feel that the less we know about this operation, the better it might be for us? We're not exactly the world's front runners in matters of politics and diplomacy, you know.'

She had a point, Martin admitted to himself grudgingly. And he had nothing to counter it with.

His silence evinced the faintest glint of triumph in the girl's eyes.

'So to answer your original question, Lieutenant-Colonel, yes I was taking some time off, and as it happens I was about to go out and watch Randy doing his windsurfing course.' Selina broke off to smile sweetly. 'Perhaps you'd care to join me?'

She had changed, Martin realized; slipped neatly into a new and different persona as suddenly and as easily as a chameleon changes colour to melt into its environment. The aggressive, efficient career woman was gone, replaced by the girl-woman who was at the same time both totally innocent and totally feminine.

It was unnerving, but utterly irresistible. Like some helpless drone, Martin allowed her to link her arm into his and lead him out towards the beach.

23

'Flashy little bastard,' Crewes spat out, his face contorted with pure hatred.

Willerbey followed his companions's eye out over the sea, to where Randy Havilland was just completing a series of rapid and extremely slick port and starboard tacks on one of Bright's boards. It looked pretty good, he thought, giving the young man credit for his skill. He couldn't quite understand why Crewes seemed to be so uptight.

'Hey, don't let it get to you,' he said. 'The guy's just good at what he does, that's all.'

Crewes remained unimpressed. 'Maybe because that's all the little tosser has to do with his fucking life,' he observed bitterly. 'Just ponce around the beaches of the world spending his daddy's money and showing off.'

Willerbey couldn't stop himself from grinning. 'I didn't know you were into all that working-class hero stuff,' he teased. 'Deprived childhood, was it? Home a cardboard box on the M1, and all that bit?'

Crewes whirled on him, his aggrieved expression fading as he saw Willerbey's grinning face. 'No, that was just the telly,' he said. 'When me mum asked for a television set, the old man put two rats in a box and cut a hole in the front. Took me three bloody years to figure out why the BBC showed nothing but wildlife programmes.'

Despite the attempt at humour, Crewes was still seething below the surface, Willerbey could tell. Perhaps it had to do with the fact that Randy made windsurfing look so easy. And perhaps also because Crewes had already had one practice session, and judging from his wet hair, had not exactly performed faultlessly.

'Didn't do too well on your test, eh?' he asked sympathetically.

Crewes glowered at him. 'Don't you bloody well start,' he warned. 'You wait until it's your turn. I tell you, those boards don't handle anything like anything else you've ever sailed. It's like trying to ride a couple of bloody planks through white water.' He nodded his head out towards Randy again. 'With that smug bastard posing about and looking down his fucking nose at you. Do you know what the arrogant little shit called me? A plonker. I nearly topped the bastard.'

'We all got called a lot worse on basic training,' Willerbey reminded him.

Anger flared in Crewes' eyes again. 'Yeah, but that was by people you could respect.' He was about to say more, but he had noticed Martin and Selina walking down the beach towards them. 'Anyway, let's drop it. Here comes the boss with the bastard's little lady-love.'

It all dropped into place. Simple jealousy, Willerbey thought. It was no secret among the men that Crewes had fancied Selina from the moment they had arrived at the Samos base.

'So that's it,' Willerbey muttered. 'You've got it in for him because he's poking the home help.'

It was meant as a gentle taunt, but the brief look of rage which crossed Crewes' face told Willerbey that he had taken it a lot harder. For a moment, he thought the man was going to explode, but then he controlled himself with a visible effort. 'I told you, just drop it,' Crewes hissed, and lapsed into a sullen silence.

Martin and Selina had reached the water's edge. Noticing them, Randy brought his windsurfer round in a clean arc and headed straight for the beach. He ran the board straight up on to the shingle, dropping the boom and jumping off in one smooth movement without even getting his white deck shoes wet. The manoeuvre was obviously well practised and designed to look good – and clearly executed for Selina's benefit.

Crewes had a point, Willerbey reflected. The man was a flash bastard. He could see potential problems if he managed to antagonize the rest of the men as easily as he had upset Crewes. Perhaps a discreet word in Martin's ear might not go amiss, he thought.

After exchanging a few words with Martin, Randy looked over and noticed Willerbey and Crewes. Excusing himself, he loped across the beach towards them, grinning amiably.

'Right, you haven't been out yet, have you?' he asked Willerbey. 'Want to show me what you can do, or are you another one with two left feet like your mate here?'

The tension could have been cut with a knife. Willerbey could almost feel his companion struggling to contain himself, straining like a dog on a leash. He took a step forward, nodding curtly at Randy. 'Yeah, let's go,' he said urgently, trying to defuse the situation as quickly as possible.

It wasn't going to work. The last little dig had pushed Crewes over the edge. Stepping directly in front of Randy, the Marine confronted him face to face, anger blazing in his eyes.

'Listen, sonny boy,' he hissed, quietly but with a chilling edge. 'You ever call me a plonker again and I'll knock every one of your pretty white capped teeth down the back of your fucking throat.'

To Willerbey's surprise, Randy didn't even flinch. The young man obviously had more guts than he had given him credit for. As he faced up squarely to Crewes' challenge there was no trace of apology in his voice.

'No, you listen to me,' he said quietly and evenly. 'I've been given a job to do – which makes you my responsibility. These boards are a bitch to handle and your lives are going to depend on them. If you can't control them fifty yards off a beach, on a nice sunny afternoon with nothing more than a breeze blowing, then how the fuck do you think you're going to manage at night, on the open sea and in the teeth of a force seven?' He paused to draw breath. 'So I'll use every trick in the book – including a few friendly jibes – to get you as proficient as I can. If you're not man enough to take it, don't come bloody whinging to me.'

Having said his piece, Randy turned on his heel and began to walk away, leaving Crewes speechless. Willerbey hurried after him, catching him up.

'That was a bit strong,' he said, his tone carrying a note of admiration rather than censure. The man had suddenly gone up several points in his estimation.

Randy shrugged and said: 'All this macho "we're the big bad tough guys" shit pisses me off. I find it arrogant.'

Willerbey smiled. 'Funny, that's what he said about you.' A sudden thought struck him. There was something which Randy had said which had struck a jarring note. 'How did you know we'd be using these things at night, anyway?'

There was the briefest moment of hesitation before Randy answered. 'Somebody must have mentioned it,' he said, trying to shrug the question off. 'Or maybe I just assumed it.'

There was nothing he could actually put his finger on, but suddenly Willerbey had the strangest feeling that the young man was lying. And, at the same time, the suspicion that Randy Havilland knew a lot more about the details of Operation Windswept than he was supposed to.

*   *   *

Martin was about to retire for the night when there was a furious pounding on his door. Throwing a shirt and trousers back on, he crossed the room and opened it to find an extremely agitated Mike Bright standing outside.

'Look, I thought I'd better come and tell you right away,' Bright blurted out. 'But one of the new rigs has gone missing.'

The information hit Martin like a bucket of cold water. He practically pulled Bright into the room, and slammed the door. 'What the hell do you mean – gone missing?'

'I mean somebody's taken one,' Bright expanded. 'The whole bloody thing. It's one of the ones Randy was using this afternoon for lessons. It was still completely rigged up.'

'Jesus Christ,' Martin groaned. He took a breath, forcing himself to remain calm and logical. He consulted his watch quickly. It was ten to eleven. 'When would it have been taken? Got any idea?'

Bright nodded. 'It must have been in the last half hour. I was working on the two newest hulls until ten, and all three of the rigged boards were stacked inside the workshop door when I left. I came back to the common room, had a nightcap and then went back to lock up. That's when I saw the rig was missing.'

A blaze of anger surfaced briefly above Martin's worries. 'You mean the place was left unlocked?'

Bright was apologetic. 'I realized I'd forgotten – that's why I went back. It was thirty-five minutes at the most.'

Martin controlled his annoyance, letting it go. There was nothing to be gained now from recriminations. He looked away and thought quickly about the best plan of action, then turned to Bright again.

'Look, I want you to round up your colleagues and assemble in the common room,' he snapped. 'Wait there until I get back and don't go outside under any circumstances. Understand?'

'OK,' Bright said with a nod. He moved towards the door, with Martin close on his heels.

Reaching the outside, Martin ran down the beach, finally intercepting Sergeant Graham, who was sharing patrol duties with Andy Donnelly. He gave the man a quick run-down on the situation, then asked: 'See anything?'

Graham shook his head. 'Not a thing, boss.'

Martin hadn't expected any other answer. The men would have already reported in if they had noticed anything suspicious. 'Right,' he snapped. 'Get back inside and shake everyone out. I want this entire base in a state of full alert – pronto.'

'Got you, boss.' The man responded at once, running back to the villas and leaving Martin to wait for Donnelly.

Crewes was also missing, along with his wetsuit. To Martin it seemed logical to assume that the two disappearances were related. What didn't make sense was why. He faced the assembled men with a look of bemusement on his face. 'Any ideas, gentlemen?'

Willerbey hesitated before speaking up. As the only witness to the exchange between Crewes and

Randy earlier in the day, he had a pretty good theory but wasn't sure whether to voice it or not. Torn between duty to his commanding officer and a sense of loyalty to a friend, he sought the compromise which would best serve both. On balance, it seemed best to tell the truth, he decided. Crewes was already in trouble, and his information could not make it worse. In fact, it might just help a little, if Martin chose to see his actions as personal initiative rather than disobedience.

'I think I might know what's happened,' Willerbey said, speaking up. He went on to outline the background. 'My guess is that young Havilland's taunts stung him deeper than either of us realized,' he concluded. 'I suppose he's just taken that rig out tonight and he won't come back until he gets it right.'

Martin felt a certain degree of relief, although he was still angry. At least the explanation pieced together logically, and if true, appeared to preclude any external and more sinister interpretation. There was only one aspect of the matter which remained unresolved. He turned to Graham and Donnelly. 'But wouldn't you two have seen him?' he demanded.

Donnelly looked slightly apologetic. 'Not if he didn't want to be seen, boss,' he pointed out. 'He could have waited until we were at opposite ends of the beach, then ran straight through the middle of us and launched. He probably paddled the board out of sight before he brought the sail up. He would have been gone in a matter of minutes.'

Martin nodded to himself. Again the explanation seemed logical. If anyone was going to get past an SBS patrol, it was another SBS man. And Crewes was good at his job. One of the best. So the mystery appeared to be solved, he thought. He had one last word for Donnelly and Graham before dismissing the rest of the men.

'Just tell Crewes to report to my quarters the minute he gets back,' he said darkly.

The trouble was, Crewes didn't get back. A search party, sent out in the Rigid Raider at first light, recovered the board and rig drifting about two hundred yards offshore, some three miles further up the coast. It appeared undamaged and in working order, but there was no sign of Crewes. They swept the entire area for the rest of the day, but to no avail.

It fell to Martin to break the inescapable conclusion to the men at another hastily convened evening meeting. His face was tired and drawn as he made the announcement.

'For the moment, Crewes will be simply listed as "missing",' he said gravely. 'But I think we must assume him to have been drowned.' Martin sighed deeply. 'That will be all, gentlemen.'

The men all filed out of the common room, with the exception of Willerbey. Martin looked at the man morosely for a few moments before asking: 'Was there something else?'

Willerbey nodded. 'I just can't bring myself to believe that he drowned,' he stated emphatically.

'John was one of the strongest swimmers I've ever known. That man would have swum home from the wreck of the *Titanic*.'

Martin nodded sadly. 'I know,' he said. 'But perhaps he didn't have a chance to swim for it. If he hit his head on the board as he fell, he could have been unconscious when he went in the water.' He paused to look at Willerbey curiously. 'Why, do you have some other theory?'

The man looked uncertain. 'Just a long shot, boss, but suppose he ran into some of the friends of our earlier visitors?'

'Yes,' Martin said with a heavy sigh. 'That thought had occurred to me too.'

After Willerbey had left the room, the CO sat alone with his thoughts for a good half hour. They were not good thoughts. In his mind a sense of anger fought for supremacy over gnawing worry. Losing a good man because of such a stupid and preventable accident was bad enough, but now the mission itself was in real jeopardy. What little margin for error Operation Windswept had ever had was being whittled away day by day.

Anger finally won the battle. Martin rose from his seat, striding across the room and slamming his bunched fist against the wall with a bitter curse. It didn't make him feel any better. He crossed to the drinks cabinet and poured himself half a tumbler of Scotch. Martin didn't normally drink when he was in the middle of an operation, but tonight he felt like getting drunk.

24

Word had got around between Martin's men about the source of the engines, so, with typical SBS black humour, the nickname 'The Flying Lawnmower' had stuck.

Now, fully assembled for the first time on the top of the headland overlooking the bay and ready for its first test, the craft appeared even less aerodynamic than its namesake. A crazy geometry of irregular angles, struts and bracing cords, the machine looked unbelievably flimsy, hardly capable of supporting the engine and the rear-mounted propeller, which seemed to have been added as an afterthought. The transparent wings only served to accentuate this skeletal appearance, inspiring little confidence that they could provide enough lift to get the twin sections of the sailboard hull off the ground, let alone a pilot as well.

Basically, it looked like something which might have been doodled on the back of a schoolboy's exercise book, but Mallory seemed proud of it. Having served as packhorses to manhandle the various component parts up to their present site,

Williams and Graham eyed the machine appre-
hensively as the American busied himself fussing
about and making final assembly adjustments.

'Jesus, can you honestly believe this fucking thing
is going to fly?' Graham asked his companion.

Williams shot him a grin. 'It'd bloody well better.
It's obviously no fucking good for cutting grass
any more.'

The two men giggled nervously as Mallory made
what appeared to be the final adjustment to the
rigging and stood back to admire his creation.
Martin, who had been hovering in the background,
stepped forward to join him.

'Everything set?'

Mallory nodded, an almost resigned expression
on his face. 'She's all ready to go. This is the bit
where pure theory goes out the window. Now we
find out if this bird is an osprey – or an ostrich!'

The light-hearted comment did nothing to dis-
sipate the tension in the air. It was crunch time,
and both men were fully aware of the fact.

'Now you're sure you want to test-fly this thing
yourself?' Martin asked, a trifle uncertainly. 'I can
ask for a volunteer to take her up for the first time
if you'd prefer.'

Mallory affected a brave grin. 'Thanks for the
offer, but I already booked my ticket in advance.'
It was his way of saying that he had test-flown
every craft he had ever designed, and the Flying
Lawnmower would be no exception to this sense
of personal responsibility. He gave his bizarre contraption another fond once-over, then turned back

to Martin. 'Actually, there is one thing you can do
for me. Have your men hold on to the wing-tips
while I start the engine, would you?'

'Sure,' Martin said, passing the instruction to
Williams and Graham. The two men took up position either side of the machine, holding it firmly
in place as Mallory ducked beneath the wings and
began to strap himself into the flying harness. Ready
to fire up the engine, he glanced back at Martin
with a slightly nervous smile on his face.

'Don't you guys have a special saying for a time
like this?' he asked. 'Do or die? Shit or bust?'

Martin smiled back. 'Sink or swim,' he confided. 'Although in your case that's not particularly
apt, is it?'

Mallory didn't answer him. He started the engine,
allowing it to tick over for a few seconds before
revving it up and down gently a few times. Satisfied
that it was running smoothly, he began to pull up
the craft's nose, yelling out to Graham and Williams
above the grating roar of the engine.

'Ok, let her go and stand clear.'

The two Marines obeyed without hesitation,
and with a certain amount of relief. Just standing
there, the machine had a certain forbidding quality
about it. Now, powered up, the throbbing engine
caused the entire structure to chatter and vibrate
like some monstrous and malevolent dragonfly.
They retreated a good six feet either side of the
wings as Mallory brought the nose up into the
neutral position and poised himself to take a run
at the edge of the headland.

The engine revved up with a rasping, high-pitched noise which suggested something like ten thousand pigs farting inside an echo-chamber. Mallory began his run forward – straight towards the sheer drop-off point which would take him out over the beach some sixty feet below.

It was a bitch of a launch, but Mallory had been expecting it and was prepared. Normally he would have equipped any microlight with a much more powerful engine, capable of taking off in much the same way as any conventional aircraft. The limitations of this particular design had not allowed for such luxury, however, providing merely enough power for thrust but little else.

So he was more or less committed to a drop launch. Leaping out over the edge of the cliff, Mallory felt his stomach lurch sickeningly as he and the entire weight of the machine plummeted like a stone for nearly fifteen feet. Then the flaccid sails above his head cracked with a surge of uprushing air and billowed into shape. The sense of weight above him seemed to disappear. He was airborne, holding height, and the Lawnmower was in level flight.

Mallory eased back on the A-frame, exchanging upward lift for a little more forward speed. Revving the engine to its full capacity, he took the machine down in a long, shallow dive to around twenty feet and then tried to level her up again before heading out over the open sea.

The craft refused to respond. Dropping more rapidly now, with the increased power from the engine, the nose remained steadfastly down. The machine continued on an angle of descent which would take it nose-diving into the Aegean in just over twelve seconds.

Mallory made one last attempt to bring the nose up by thrusting the A-frame away from his body with all his strength. There was a marginal decrease in the angle of dive, but not enough to prevent disaster. In desperation, he cut the engine back to idling power, flying the craft like an ordinary hang-glider. She came up sluggishly but surely, pulling into level flight again with the flotation boards virtually skimming the surface of the sea. Mallory increased power again, gently, fighting to hold the craft in the air long enough to build up to sufficient power for a gradual climb.

It was touch and go for nearly half a minute as Mallory nursed the unwieldy contraption over the surface of the sea, pulling back on the motor-cycle style accelerator grip mounted on the control bar a centimetre at a time. Finally, he was two feet clear of the water – then three – and the Lawnmower was climbing steadily at an angle of about fifteen degrees.

Having taken her up to around fifty feet, Mallory banked the machine round in a rather ponderous ninety-degree turn and headed back towards the beach, making a series of zigzagging course changes all the way. Finally cutting the engine some fifty yards short of the shoreline, he allowed the craft to take its own natural angle of glide and let it flop gently down on to the surface of the water about ten feet from the beach and float smoothly on to the shingle.

Lindbergh himself could not have been treated to a more enthusiastic reception upon landing. Lieutenant-Colonel Martin, Williams and Graham had already made their way down to the beach from the launch point, where they had been joined by the rest of the men, Bright and Janice and even Pavlaski. Selina and Randy had been watching the flight too, but from a detached, somewhat aloof position over by the villas, sharing a pair of powerful binoculars.

The assembled reception committee broke into a ragged chorus of cheers, whistles and shouts of congratulation as Mallory unstrapped his harness and pulled the Lawnmower up on to the beach.

The pilot, however, did not appear to share their enthusiasm. He walked up the beach away from the machine, his face set.

Martin detached himself from the crowd and hurried to Mallory's side. 'Problems?' he asked, his tone betraying a note of concern.

Mallory chewed his lower lip. He looked almost worried – and certainly disappointed. 'She's a real mean bitch,' he said gloomily. 'Even worse reponse than I feared, and it's virtually impossible to make any degree of flight rotation with the engine at anything over half power. There ain't an ounce of forgiveness in her.'

'It looked all right to me,' Martin said, trying to inject a more optimistic note into the conversation.

Mallory grunted. 'It might have *looked* all right. It felt like shit.'

Martin was thoughtful for a second. 'Is there anything you can do? A bit of fine-tuning, perhaps?'

Mallory shook his head slowly. 'Not without going right back to the drawing board, and we don't have time for that, do we?' He stared at the ground for a long time, then said: 'Basically, what you see is what you've got. She's lumpy, cumbersome, and she leaves absolutely no margin for error. The pilot makes one single mistake, and he's fucked.'

'But it flies,' Martin pointed out. There didn't seem to be very much more that he could say.

Mallory let out a short, bitter snort. 'Yeah, so does a fucking chicken.'

He'd had enough, Martin decided. It was time to be more positive. 'Look, we weren't expecting Concorde,' he pointed out. 'Right from the start we agreed this thing was going to be a bad compromise at the best. The worst of both worlds, I believe were your own words.' He looked hard at Mallory. 'This is right on the line – will that machine make the flight to the distance and specifications we originally discussed?'

The American's response was somewhat evasive. 'Will it, or could it?' he replied. 'There's a difference.'

It was a hell of a time to be arguing over semantics, Martin thought rather testily, but it seemed the only way forward. He decided to humour the man. 'OK then – could it?' he said in a tone of exaggerated patience.

Mallory nodded faintly. 'With a lot of luck and everything going in our favour, yes, I'd say that the original objectives remained a distinct possibility,' he admitted grudgingly.

'And you can teach my men how to handle it, learn to compensate for its performance flaws?' Martin pressed, eager to build on the American's slim concession.

Another guarded nod preceded Mallory's response. 'To a certain degree, yes. But don't forget that I've only flown the damn thing for five minutes myself so far. God only knows what other little bugs are likely to show up when we start testing it under more difficult conditions.' His eyes narrowed slightly. 'To be perfectly frank, man, I can't help feeling you're either ignoring or deliberately evading the real issue here.'

'Which is?' Martin asked.

Mallory nodded over towards the Lawnmower, standing by the water's edge. 'Try to remember what we're actually dealing with here,' he urged. 'That contraption is a highly unstable, potentially lethal piece of experimental machinery. If we manage to get through any sort of training programme at all without a serious accident, it'll be nothing short of a miracle. And I was never a great believer in miracles.'

Martin smiled wistfully. 'Nor I, Mr Mallory. But I wasn't evading the point, believe me. I can assure you that I'm fully aware of the dangers involved here.'

'Yes, I'm sure you are,' Mallory conceded. 'But

are you really prepared to take that sort of responsibility on your shoulders?' It was a pointless question. Mallory knew the answer even as he spoke the words.

'I'm afraid I don't have the luxury of choice,' Martin replied firmly. 'It goes with the territory. Surely you understand that?'

The American stared at him glumly for a few seconds, nodding faintly to himself. 'Yeah,' he sighed. 'And I'm sorry to have to pile even more weight on the load you're already carrying, but it needs to be said.'

'So say it, and get it off your chest.'

'In my opinion, if you continue with this project someone is going to get killed,' Mallory said bluntly.

Martin accepted the man's opinion with a look of blank stoicism. 'Someone already has,' he said solemnly, thinking of John Crewes.

25

Two weeks later, Mallory's dire prophecies mercifully remained unfulfilled, although there had been two near misses in which disaster was only split seconds away. One incident involved Willerbey, who was still having trouble mastering the drop-launch technique, and the other Mallory himself, while trying to coerce the Lawnmower into an impossibly tight 360-degree turn. The American seemed hell-bent on pushing the machine far beyond the limits of what would actually be required of it, Martin had decided. He could only assume that there was a bit of the daredevil lurking in the heart of every flyer.

Surprisingly, it was Donnelly who had quickly proved himself to be the most adept pilot, even though he had actually logged up the least previous flight hours of the whole group. It was Mallory's contention that this lack of experience was actually an advantage when dealing with a machine like the Flying Lawnmower, since he was less preconditioned to expect more conventional flight characteristics and performance.

There were now three fully airworthy machines,

with one more completely assembled but awaiting the wings from Janice. Mallory was about to make a start on the fifth and final machine, which Martin estimated would put them about two days ahead of the original schedule. Things were going well and then the shit hit the fan.

The phone call came in on a Code I security channel patched in through Cyprus, so Martin had a nasty fluttering feeling in his gut even before he picked up the receiver. The Foreign Secretary's opening words turned the butterflies into vampire bats.

'Lieutenant-Colonel Martin? I'm afraid we have something of a problem.'

The voice betrayed the faintest hint of an apology. Martin took a deep breath before responding. 'How big a problem?' he asked flatly.

The Foreign Secretary coughed gently down the line. 'That rather depends on your situation. How far advanced are your plans over there?'

'Very slightly ahead of schedule,' Martin said guardedly, suddenly having a premonition of what was coming. In the event it proved to be uncannily accurate.

'Good,' the Foreign Secretary said with evident relief. 'Because it looks as if the schedule has changed. Our latest intelligence reports that the Russians may be planning to ship the consignment out ten days earlier than we reckoned.'

Martin allowed himself the indulgence of a groan. 'Why the sudden change of plan? Or was it faulty intelligence in the first place?'

The Foreign Secretary was quick to deny the second suggestion. 'No, we have absolutely no cause to doubt our original information. But now there seems to be an additional factor which has changed things. It would appear that the Russians have got wind of something, and it seems to have somewhat spooked them.' He broke off, hastening to reassure Martin and correct any wrong impression he might have given. 'Oh, nothing directly connected with Operation Windswept, I assure you. We are convinced that our security on that is still one hundred per cent. This is something else they seem to have picked up, although it might be related in some way. We're investigating, and of course you'll be the first to know if we find anything out.'

'All right, you've told me the cause. Now what's the effect?' Martin asked.

'It seems our Russian friends are having second thoughts about the sensitivity and value of this particular cargo,' the Foreign Secretary went on. 'They've brought forward the shipping date to coincide with some genuine naval exercises which will be taking place in the area. The effect, besides advancing the schedule, is that the freighter will now have a much bigger shadowing escort for much of its journey.'

'How much bigger?' Martin asked warily.

'Probably up to twenty surface ships and at least one submarine. There could be a fair amount of air activity in the region as well.'

It was about as bad as it could get, Martin

thought, short of dispatching the entire Russian fleet. 'So what's the bad news?' he asked wryly.

The Foreign Secretary let out a faint snort, which could have been a restrained laugh or annoyance. Martin wasn't sure which, and realized he didn't really care.

'I'm glad to see that you are able to retain a sense of humour, Lieutenant-Colonel,' the Foreign Secretary said. 'Now, the crunch is simply this: can you meet this new deadline? Is your equipment ready, for a start?'

Martin had been expecting the question, but it still shook him. He was quietly thoughtful for a while. 'Yes, the equipment is ready, or it will be,' he admitted at last. 'But my men certainly aren't. They've only just got into their training programmes, and we haven't even started on ship-board familiarization sessions with Pavlaski.'

'But these things have already been scheduled?' the Foreign Secretary probed.

Martin could feel the pressure increasing, and felt uncomfortable. 'Yes, sir, they're scheduled,' he admitted grudgingly. 'But over a period of three weeks. What hasn't even been scheduled yet is the hours of practice they're going to need to learn how to dismantle and convert the machines from one mode to another. We haven't even rehearsed the procedure yet, let alone attempted it at night, on the open sea. The men simply are not fully prepared, and I don't think there's any way that they could be in that time-span.'

'Then you'll just have to step up your training

schedules,' the Foreign Secretary said coldly, as if Martin's objections carried no weight at all.

It took a few seconds for the full implication of the man's words to sink into Martin's brain, but when it did so he felt his hackles rising.

'Now wait a minute, sir,' he blurted out, his voice rising as he fought to control his temper. 'You promised me I had total discretion over this mission.'

There was a momentary silence at the other end of the line. 'I'm sorry, Lieutenant-Colonel Martin,' the Foreign Secretary said finally, and the apology sounded genuine. 'Circumstances have changed.'

'Damn right they have,' Martin said bitterly. Seething with anger, he took a few moments to try to come to terms with the welter of thoughts fighting in his head. It went against every grain of his being to even consider scrubbing a mission, but on the other hand his first consideration had to be for the safety of his men. Taking a deep breath, he made a direct appeal to the Foreign Secretary.

'Sir, may I put something on record at the present time?'

'Of course.'

'I fought for this operation every step of the way. And I am fully aware both of its importance and of the huge investment of money and manpower which has gone into it. However, it is my opinion that these changed circumstances now place it in extreme jeopardy. I believe it would be suicidal to send my men in under these conditions. It is my considered judgement, therefore,

that Operation Windswept should be aborted forth-
with.'

The Foreign Secretary sighed. 'Your opinions
are noted, Lieutenant-Colonel, and I sympathize
with them. However, I'm afraid that this matter
has now gone over both our heads. This mission
will proceed as planned, and that's a direct order
from the very top.'

'Then you're getting your orders from a totally
irresponsible bloody prat,' Martin exploded.

The Foreign Secretary coughed suddenly, as
though he were trying to cover something else up.
'Indeed, that's more than possible,' he murmured,
then hung up.

Martin slammed the receiver back into its cradle
in a futile gesture of rage. Rising to his feet, he paced
up and down the small room fretfully, marshalling
his thoughts. Faced with a *fait accompli*, he could
only make the best of a bad job, and plan accord-
ingly. If Windswept was going to go ahead against
his advice, then it would at least do so with every
possible bit of help he could give it.

Returning to his desk, Martin sat down again
and started making detailed plans.

26

There was no point in beating about the bush, Martin thought; and he knew and trusted his men enough to respect their right to be given the facts upfront. So his opening address to the hastily convened meeting was brief and to the point.

'As of this morning, gentlemen, this entire base goes on a sixteen-hour day. The clock just ran out on us.'

He paused to let the expected ripple of groans and grumbles ripple around the room. It was almost a convention, a ritual. Each of the men would feign their individual protest or complaint, make a momentary play of rebellion, then become part of a cohesive unit again, ready to knuckle down to the job, whatever its demands. They always did.

'So who cocked up this time, boss?' Williams called out. 'Them or us?'

Martin smiled at the man indulgently, spelling out the basic facts as he understood them. 'So, basically we now have just over one week instead of three,' he finished off. 'We're going to have to get our skates on.'

He crossed to the notice-board and pinned up

a large diagram of the Russian freighter which Pavlaski had drawn up. It was fairly basic, intended only to show the general layout of decks and cargo areas, but it would do for a preliminary briefing. The Russian would join them to discuss the specifics later, when they had got other business out of the way.

'Nice drawing, boss. Who's the artist?' Graham asked. Martin ignored him. Taking up a pointer, he tapped the sketch roughly amidships.

'This is your target,' he announced. 'Our intelligence sources say that she'll be a 12,000-tonner of the Poltava class, with aft-mounted bridge, radio shack, engine-rooms and crew quarters.' Martin paused. 'So you're going to have to be bloody gentle when you place those magnetic clamps. Let them slam against the outside of the hull and you might as well radio them to tell them you're coming.'

'Then why don't we go up over the side?' Willerbey asked. 'That way we'd be nearer to the cargo hatches to start with.'

Martin shook his head. 'Too risky. You're going to have to make sure you've knocked out the radio and neutralized the bridge crew before you venture out on to the deck area. The only logical way is to come up on them from behind.'

'Neutralize, boss?' Williams asked. 'I take it we're not supposed to do any of the Russkis any permanent damage?'

'That is paramount,' Martin confirmed, with heavy emphasis. 'Under no circumstances are you to use more force than is strictly necessary to overpower any opposition you might come up against. Remember, this is a merchant vessel and we're not at war. I shouldn't need to remind any of you of the sort of shit which would hit the fan if any civilian got killed.' Martin paused again, before delivering the punchline. 'For that reason alone, you will all be going in unarmed.'

He had expected a fairly shocked reaction, and he got it. He waited patiently as the sudden and animated buzz of conversation died down.

'Not even side-arms?' Graham asked, as though he couldn't quite believe it. Asking an SBS Marine to go anywhere without some kind of weapon was almost like pulling the spines out of a hedgehog.

Martin shook his head. 'Not even a bloody penknife,' he said emphatically.' You will all be issued with a coil of wire and a roll of sticky tape. You will bind and gag any crew members you are forced to take out, rendering them unconscious if necessary.'

'And if we have to fight our way out of a tight spot? If it's a case of one of them or one of us? What then?' Williams asked.

'It mustn't happen,' Martin said flatly. 'If you're pinned down, your first objective will be to try and escape. If that is impossible, you will be expected to surrender.'

Another angry buzz filled the room. The men weren't at all happy, Martin could see, and he fully understood their fears. They were being asked to undertake a dangerous mission with one hand tied behind their backs. It was against everything they

had been trained and conditioned for, and totally
outside their normal field of experience, so it was
no wonder they didn't like the idea.

'So what are we likely to be up against?' Williams
asked finally. It was a fairly obvious and perfectly
reasonable question, under the circumstances.

'Pavlaski assures me that no Russian merchant
personnel carry weapons as a matter of course,'
Martin announced. 'However, the skipper and first
mate will most probably have access to a small store
of firearms secured under lock and key. It will be
up to you to ensure that they do not get a chance
to break them out.'

'Numbers?' Corporal Bailey asked.

'The ship would normally carry a complement
of fifty-five crew members, of whom a couple of
dozen might be expected to be above decks at any
one time. However, at the time you'll be going in,
it's reasonable to assume that there should be no
more than six crew on night watch – plus the
captain or first officer, of course. Hopefully, the
bulk of the crew will be either asleep or stoned
out of their brains on vodka. The sleeping quarters
are well away from the cargo area, so you shouldn't
have any trouble if you get that far cleanly.' Martin
paused, surveying his men expectantly. 'Now, any
other questions before we get down to the actual
attack plan?'

The offer was greeted with a strained silence,
which Martin took as his invitation to carry on.

'Right, so your primary objective will be to knock
out the radio and neutralize the bridge,' he told

them. 'If that freighter manages to get a message out, then the Russian Navy is going to be down on you like a ton of bricks in a matter of minutes. With that accomplished, you will overpower any remaining members of the watch crew and make your way to the main cargo hatches and effect an entry. You will take two samples of the guidance system, encasing them in the special waterproof packs you will each be issued with.'

Martin broke off for a moment, drawing a breath. 'And one last, and very important instruction,' he added. 'Before leaving the ship, you will ensure that at least one crew member is capable of freeing himself within a maximum of five minutes. It will not be practical to stop the freighter in mid-ocean without arousing suspicion, and we dare not risk causing a maritime disaster by allowing a crewless vessel to continue ploughing through the night. I'm afraid it won't give you a great deal of time to get away before they start looking for you, but you'll be very small targets on a very big sea and if everything goes to schedule you should still have at least two hours of darkness left for cover. With a bit of luck you should be able to reach Cypriot waters by first light and your pick-up operation will already be underway. Now, any other questions at this stage?'

'Yes, when we get into the cargo hold how do we know what we're looking for?' Willerbey asked. 'It'd be a shame to go through all this and come away with two cases of beluga caviar.'

Martin allowed himself a thin smile. 'You shouldn't

have any trouble there,' he assured the man. 'Our intelligence tells us that the vessel will only be carrying heavy artillery and tank equipment besides the guidance systems, and all that will be in large container modules. The units we're after will be individually crated and should be about the size of a small attaché case. You will, of course, break one open to check its contents before you leave.'

Martin turned back to the diagram. 'Now, I want all of you to familiarize yourselves thoroughly with this rough layout and put together any more detailed questions you might want to ask Pavlaski. I'm confident that Sergeant Graham's Russian will be more than adequate for translation purposes. In the meantime, I shall be working out your training schedules for the next few days. We're all going to be rather busy little bees.'

It was an understatement, but Martin had no intention of communicating any negative thoughts to the men. He still had grave doubts about their ability to compress the work required into the time available. To even approach the degree of intensive preparation required was going to place them all under almost intolerable strain.

But each man would find that out for himself soon enough, Martin thought. There was no point in spelling it out in advance. They would all need every ounce of confidence as an inner reserve if they were to stand a snowball's chance in hell of succeeding.

27

Lieutenant-Colonel Martin escorted the party of civilians towards the waiting minibus with mixed feelings. He would be lying to himself if he pretended he wasn't both relieved and anxious to finally get rid of them. Working with them in the first place had gone against every instinct of his military training and background, and now that Mission Day had finally arrived, the sooner they were away from the base the better. On the other hand, he felt a genuine debt of gratitude for their help and cooperation and wished that their hastily enforced departure was not quite so awkward.

To dismiss them without a word of thanks seemed churlish. Reaching the side of the bus, he turned to face them stiffly, holding out his hand in a rather self-conscious gesture.

'Well, I can only say, thank you,' he said, after clearing his throat noisily.

Janice accepted the proffered hand first. She smiled up at Martin sweetly. 'Poor man, this has all been a terrible strain for you, hasn't it? No wonder you can't wait to get rid of us.'

Martin found himself flushing with embarrassment. He had been fondly imagining that his inner feelings weren't quite so obvious. He tried to mumble some sort of denial, but nothing came out. He could only gape after Janice dumbly as she climbed on to the bus.

Bright shook his hand curtly, as if aware that the gesture was a mere concession to courtesy. Martin felt an obligation to open some kind of conversation, however brief.

'I hope you don't feel your time here has been entirely wasted, Mr Bright. Your efforts will be invaluable, I assure you.'

Bright smiled. 'Oh, I've gained a few new ideas from the experience,' he said casually. 'Although somehow I don't think there's going to be a great deal of commercial potential to be exploited here.' He followed Janice up the steps of the bus.

Mallory turned towards the headland, where the five microlights stood ready assembled, minus only the wings. He took a last, lingering glance at his creations before turning back to Martin, a wistful smile on his lips. 'I suppose we'll never know what happens to them?' He already knew the answer.

Martin shook his head slowly. 'It's not something you'll be able to read about in the Sunday papers,' he murmured.

Mallory nodded thoughtfully to himself. 'Yeah, that's what I figured,' he said as he took Martin's hand in a firm handshake. 'Well, I hope they do the job you wanted them for — whatever that is.'

Martin stepped aside as the American pushed

past him, directing his attention to Randy, who was standing uncertainly a few yards from the bus, staring towards the cluster of villas. He looked slightly worried.

'Forgotten something, Mr Havilland?' Martin asked.

Randy looked at him morosely. 'It's just that I expected Selina to say goodbye,' he murmured. 'But I haven't seen her all morning.'

The observation stirred something in the back of Martin's mind. It was odd, he realized suddenly, but he hadn't seen the girl that morning, either. And it certainly seemed strange that she should not wish to bid farewell to Havilland, after the closeness of their friendship. He called over to Bailey, posted outside the villas.

'Corporal, have you seen Miss Tsigarides this morning?'

'She's not here, sir,' the Marine shot back, adopting a more formal tone in front of civilians. 'She went into Samos Town early yesterday evening and didn't return. I thought you knew.'

'No, I didn't,' Martin said distractedly. He turned back to Randy, his face apologetic. 'I'm sorry, Mr Havilland, but I had no idea that Selina had other business to attend to.'

The young man looked bitterly disappointed. Bending to heft up his suitcase, he trudged miserably towards the bus and climbed aboard as the driver started the engine.

Martin watched the bus as it disappeared into the olive grove and began to wind up the hill away from the villas. He turned back towards the villas, trying to push any doubts about Selina's disappearance from his mind. There were far more important things to worry about. It was going to be a busy day.

Selina had not returned by the time dusk began to fall, but by then Martin had already ceased to concern himself about her. Her presence was, after all, no longer strictly necessary. Her job was done, and she had already set in motion all the elements of cooperation with the Greek authorities. The homing beacon was already in place on the Russian freighter and transmitting a clear signal on a frequency which the Russian naval ships would have no reason to monitor. The girl had served her purpose, and once his team was on its way in a matter of a few minutes now, there would be nothing more that anyone could do anyway.

Martin checked his watch. It was just after 9.45. He strolled outside, staring out across the beach. The top crescent of the sun was still visible above the gaudy red and orange mirror of the sea. In another two minutes it would have sunk below the horizon, and night would start to close in. It would be a good night, he thought with a sense of relief. The skies had been clear all day, with a moderate if occasionally gusty wind blowing steadily from the east. The moon had entered a fresh cycle only three days earlier, so bright moonlight would not be a problem. All in all, conditions for the mission were about as near perfect as he could have hoped for.

The men who would be going on it were still sleeping. After a last, frenzied training session in the morning, Martin had ordered all of them to their quarters, with instructions to get as much rest as they could. They would need it. Martin thought about waking them, then took another look at the setting sun. There was a while yet, he thought. He could send Bailey, who was guarding the Flying Lawnmowers, back to shake them out. Having been dropped from the mission proper, he would probably welcome the opportunity to join in his companions' traditional bullshit as they psyched themselves up for the job ahead.

Martin began to walk briskly towards the headland, taking in great lungfuls of the cool evening air. Back in one of the villas a telephone rang, but he ignored it.

Martin had been right about the moonlight. The pale silver crescent in the dark sky threw down just enough gentle illumination to give reasonable close-range visibility, but the greater mass of the Aegean stretching out to the purple line of the horizon remained a black and featureless carpet.

The only thing no longer fully in their favour was the wind, which had become distinctly more gusty in the last half hour, veering slightly towards the north. Striking the prominence of the headland at that particular angle, it created irregular, swirling updraughts which curled up over the rim of the cliff, plucking at the flaccid wings of the waiting microlights and making them flap quite noisily.

Martin had already changed the take-off position from the original site in an effort to compensate, but conditions would still make for a particularly tricky launch. The pilots would have to make very sure they were well clear of the edge before opening up their engines, lest a sudden side gust sent them cartwheeling back against the side of the cliff.

The frequency of the gusts was increasing as the air temperature began to drop. It was time to go, Martin decided, before conditions deteriorated even further. He glanced over to the men, who were clustered in a tight knot beside the furthest Lawnmower sharing a last joke. He waited until a ripple of laughter signalled the punchline, then called out to them.

'OK, it's shake-out time,' he announced. 'Let's go cut some grass,' he added in a mock-American accent.

After a final bout of backslapping, the men moved smoothly and silently to their machines. Martin visited them each individually as they strapped themselves into their harnesses, delivering the same message.

'Good luck,' he said simply. Then he stood well back as four engines coughed into life, their concerted power shattering the silence of the night. For some unaccountable reason, Martin imagined a gang of Hell's Angels revving up for a motorcycle raid. Probably not a wildly fantastic image, he thought to himself.

The take-off sequence had already been planned

and rehearsed several times. Mallory's candid assessment of each pilot's skill was used to arrange the men in a rough order of ability, with the least competent going first. It was perhaps a rather cynical way of looking at things, but eminently practical, Martin reminded himself. With Bailey grounded because he just wasn't good enough, he was now down to four men – already one below the minimum he had deemed necessary to see the operation through with a reasonable chance of success. If a single pilot failed to launch, it would be all over, with no need to expose any remaining men to the dangers of take-off. Martin felt his stomach contract as Graham pulled up the nose of his machine and lined himself up for a run at the cliff edge. A superb glider pilot, Graham had nevertheless found it extremely difficult to adjust himself to the Flying Lawnmower's heavy and delayed responses.

Poised in position, the man waited, feeling the gusts of wind across his face and counting off the spaces in between. There was no discernible rhythm or sequence – the wind pattern was breaking up now into an almost constant series of squalls and eddies. There was no point in waiting any longer. Lowering the nose of the machine into a neutral position so that the main force of the wind broke evenly both above and below the wings, he threw himself forward.

A sudden and particularly violent updraught took him the second that he cleared the edge, pushing up the nose and inflating the wings with a sharp crack. The craft rose rapidly, the force of the wind blowing it back over the headland, above the heads of the other men. They could all see the danger. The nose was still dangerously high, and the craft's engine was still on little more than tick-over. Should the wind drop suddenly, Graham was virtually in a stall position, and desperately vulnerable.

Martin brought his hands up to his face, cupping them around his mouth like a megaphone. He screamed at the top of his voice, trying to make himself heard above the din of the engines.

'Get the nose down, man. For Christ's sake get the nose down.'

It was unlikely that Graham heard him, but in any case he chose another way to get himself out of trouble, just as effective as decreasing his angle to the wind. He opened up the throttle, allowing the engine to fire up to full power. The craft bit into the wind, arresting the backwards drift and converting into an almost vertical climb. When the wind did drop suddenly, some fifteen seconds later, he already had enough height to give him a safety margin. Bringing the machine into a shallow dive, he soared out over the headland and took up a slow, lazy circling pattern some forty feet above the surface of the sea.

It was Willerbey's turn. Although a superb natural flyer, in Mallory's estimation, he had consistently fluffed the drop-launch technique, and remained the only member of the team who had actually made a crash landing in shallow water. He'd been lucky, for only a few seconds earlier he would have plunged nose first on to the beach, probably breaking several bones in the process.

His launch this time was no less messy. A small gust caught the underside of the starboard wing as he cleared the edge of the cliff, sending the machine lurching sideways at a crazy angle. Like Graham before him, Willerbey found himself being blown back over the headland again, but without the benefit of an updraught to give him height. He did the only thing he could, wrestling the machine round in a forty-five-degree turn and levelling off to skim parallel to the beach, his wing-tip perilously close to the cliff edge. It seemed an eternity before he was finally clear, and able to fly out over the sea to join Graham.

Williams launched quickly and reasonably cleanly in his wake, although with little grace. Finally, Donnelly took to the air, with a near-flawless copy of Mallory's technique. With all four men safely airborne, Martin allowed himself to breathe normally again.

He watched the microlights circle in the night sky for a few moments, like a quartet of gigantic and unusually noisy bats. Then, raising a large torch into the air, he gave the signal that would send them on their way. The four flyers arranged themselves into a loose formation and turned their craft out to sea.

Martin stood motionless as the drone of the four engines gradually faded into silence. They were on their way, he thought – and they were on their own. There was nothing more he could do to help or protect them. He wondered briefly if a mother bird felt the same sense of anticlimax as she watched her fledglings leave the nest for the first and last time.

28

The telephone was ringing insistently as Martin walked back towards the villas. He stepped up his pace, pausing briefly beside Bailey, who was on guard duty and had an unspoken question in his eyes. The corporal smiled at him apologetically.

'Sorry, sir, it's been ringing like that for the last ten minutes, but it's on your secure line and your door is locked.'

With a tightening feeling in his gut, Martin pushed past him and made a beeline for his private quarters. He unlocked the door, strode into the room and snatched up the receiver. His feeling of unease increased as he recognized the call signal which announced that the line was being patched through GCHQ.

'Lieutenant-Colonel Martin?' enquired the male operator.

'Speaking.' There was a brief pause.

'This is a priority one,' the operator announced flatly. 'Will you please confirm that your line is secure, sir?'

Martin dropped the telephone briefly to cross to his door and lock it. He snatched up the receiver again. 'Security confirmed,' he snapped. Ten seconds later he was talking to the Foreign Secretary again.

The man seemed ill at ease. 'Where the devil have you been?' he demanded. 'I've been trying to get through to you for nearly half an hour. There have been a couple of new developments and I thought you might want to delay the launch until you were brought up to date on the situation.'

Martin's vague premonitions were now hardening into real fear. Something was terribly wrong. Unable to control himself, he let out a long, hopeless sigh. 'It's too late. They've gone, and I have absolutely no way of recalling them.'

'I see,' the Foreign Secretary said curtly. There was a long period of silence.

'My men, are they in danger?' Martin asked finally, in a tone which was both concerned and resigned at the same time.

'Perhaps not,' came the answer, but in a tone which lacked both confidence and sincerity. 'We may simply be overreacting, reading more into the situation than it warrants.'

'What situation?' Martin asked coldly.

'We've discovered what appears to have spooked the Russians,' the politician announced. 'Apparently the Israelis have been taking behind-the-scenes interest in our little project, and the Russians must have picked up some sort of a sniff from them.'

Martin didn't have the faintest idea what the man was talking about. 'What the hell have the Israelis got to do with any of this?'

'Well, they do have rather a vested interest,' the Foreign Secretary pointed out. 'Most of the missiles are pointed in their direction, after all. We suspect that their intelligence service picked up on the shipment accidentally, much in the same way as our own did. Somewhere along the line, I'm afraid it looks very much as though we got our wires crossed.'

Martin felt his temper rising. 'So this is all another cock-up by the green slime, is it?' he demanded, meaning the Intelligence Corps.

The Foreign Secretary was instantly on the defensive. 'Not entirely,' he protested. 'We've actually pinpointed the source of the leak to the Israelis as the merchant banker, Havilland senior.'

It was another piece of information which didn't appear to make any sense. 'But why would Havilland want to help the Israelis?' Martin asked. 'He's not even Jewish.'

'True, but a great many people in the world of high finance are,' the Foreign Secretary pointed out. 'The man may have been coerced or put under pressure of some kind. Or indeed it might simply be that he placed business higher on his list of priorities than receiving a knighthood. Absolutely no chance of that now, of course.'

'Oh, of course,' Martin echoed ironically. He found the Foreign Secretary's apparent flippancy totally infuriating, under the circumstances. He had just dispatched four excellent men on what could well turn out to be a suicide mission. He ran what he had learned so far through his mind, trying to make a quick assessment. 'So what you're telling me basically is that the Russians probably already know we're coming? That my men are heading straight into a trap?'

'Not necessarily. In fact, not really likely. The last thing the Israelis want to do is to actually tip the Russians off. No, I think a more realistic interpretation of the situation would be that the Russians suspect something is going on, but have no idea how, when, or from what quarter. They are obviously on their guard, but Windswept may not be compromised to any significant degree.' The man paused for a moment. 'Anyway, I'm sure you will get a much clearer picture when you interrogate your Miss Tsigarides. Our information now suggests that she is in fact a double agent, working for the Israeli Secret Service.'

With that last bombshell, it finally all fell into place, Martin realized. Selina's abrupt disappearance, the apparent closeness between her and Randy Havilland, Mallory's missing design printout – and possibly the two incursions into the cove. She may even have had something to do with the death or disappearance of Crewes as well. Now he might never know.

Martin sighed again. 'I'm afraid that will not be possible,' he answered regretfully. 'Miss Tsigarides has already flown the nest and all the civilians were returned to the mainland this morning.'

The Foreign Secretary clicked his tongue in a gesture of minor irritation. 'Oh dear,' he said with finality. 'Now that *is* most unfortunate.'

WINDSWEPT

It was the straw which broke the camel's back. Martin felt his rage welling up, fit to burst out of the top of his head like pressurized steam. He slammed the phone back into its cradle before he blurted out something he might well regret later. Still fuming, he made straight for the whisky bottle.

29

The four Flying Lawnmowers droned onward, spaced out in a rough diamond formation about thirty feet apart and some twenty feet above the sea. Having skirted round the southern tip of Rhodes roughly half an hour earlier, they were now clear of the last of the Greek islands and well into the unbroken expanse of the open Mediterranean. A good twelve miles out from the Turkish coast, there was now nothing between them and the island of Cyprus, still over a hundred miles to the east.

Mallory had been right about one thing, Willerbey thought. The prone harness might be fine for an hour of gentle hilltop soaring on a summer's afternoon; but it was bloody uncomfortable for sustained flight on a cool night over the sea. Every muscle in his body ached with cramp, and even the double skin of his neoprene wetsuit offered little protection against the seeping cold which drained away his body heat as fast as he could produce it.

It would be warmer once they ditched in the sea, he reflected. They could not have much more than twenty minutes of flying time left, and once their bodies were wet the suits could function as they were designed to, trapping an insulating layer of water between the skin and the inner layer of fabric. At least changing to the windsurfer mode would give them all the opportunity to loosen up and restore movement to their trapped and rigid bodies.

Not that the next stage would be a milk run, he realized, looking down at the turbulent surface below him. The change of waters had brought a marked difference in conditions. While the Aegean had been like a sheet of black glass, the Med was distinctly choppy, with a heavy swell and criss-crossed with the darting lines of white-topped breakers. It seemed to be getting progressively heavier the further they flew, and Willerbey estimated that they could be facing troughs of three or four feet by the time they went down.

It was not a topic he had a chance to dwell upon. Ahead of him, flying point, Graham had started to bank to port, rotating his craft into a shallow but sustained climb towards 150 feet. Staring ahead, Willerbey could see the reason. Still perhaps a mile and a half in the distance, the twinkling lights of a large ship were clearly visible. It was probably a tanker, and nothing whatsoever to do with the Russian patrol ships, Willerbey thought, but he could understand the sergeant's caution. There was no point in taking chances. He followed the man on to a course which would give the vessel a wide berth.

The lights finally dropped away behind them, and

there was only the white tops of the waves to disturb the enveloping blackness of the sea again. Following Graham's lead, the four microlights dropped down again to the twenty-foot level and resumed their former course.

The constant wall of noise which had been drumming into each pilot's head since take-off changed slightly in tone. Donnelly's engine dropped in revs, fired up to full power again for a few seconds, then spluttered and died as the carburettor sucked in nothing but vapour. Deprived of its thrust, the Flying Lawnmower sank rapidly towards the heaving waves.

Out in front, Graham had noted the change in engine noise and began a long, 360-degree sweep which would bring him back round to Donnelly's landing point. There was no need for Willerbey or Williams to make a similar manoeuvre. After cutting their own engines, they simply glided down to join their grounded companion.

On the surface of the water, the swell didn't seem quite as bad as it had looked from the air, Willerbey thought. The twin sections of the craft's landing hulls tended to damp out the worst of the wave peaks, and the troughs were at the most no more than two or three feet deep. Dismantling the Flying Lawnmowers and converting them into windsurfers would be awkward but not impossible.

The first priority was to get the four craft lashed together. While still in their microlight mode, the machines were totally at the mercy of the wind and waves, with absolutely no directional control or method of propulsion. In that highly vulnerable state, there was the distinct danger that one or all the craft could be swept away into the darkness, with little chance of ever finding one another again. Hurriedly, Willerbey uncoiled from around his waist a long length of thin but strong nylon cord which had already been weighted at one end. Holding the bulk of the coil firmly, he tossed the cord over to Donnelly, who lashed it around one of his spars and passed it on to Williams. Having completed his turn, Graham landed in the water some twenty feet behind them and taxied to join them before finally killing his engine. He tied his craft up on Willerbey's side and gently pulled the four craft as close together as possible.

Willerbey glanced over at him. 'What do you reckon, Sarge? Do we use the rest of our fuel to continue under power, or shall we strip down now?'

Graham considered the first suggestion before rejecting it. Although they could certainly use the remaining life of each engine in turn to tow the four craft along in flotilla, the plan had one major drawback: noise. The homing device they were using to close in on their target was highly accurate for bearings, but gave only a very rough idea of actual distance. They had no precise way of knowing how close they were to their quarry, nor where the shadowing Russian naval ships might be. Besides, Martin had warned them that there could well be at least one submarine in the convoy. Its sophisticated and delicate sonar gear would be able to pick up any surface noise from a range of several miles.

He shook his head. 'No, we've had our joyride. From now on we do it the hard way.' He turned towards the other two men. 'All right, let's get moving.'

On training exercises they had all managed to get the process of strip-down and conversion to well under fifteen minutes. But that had been on a comparatively calm sea. Under the present conditions, with the four craft surging up and down like horses on a merry-go-round, the job took over half an hour. Finally, however, the twin pontoons of each craft had been locked together into a single hull, the wings unzipped and converted into a sail and the engines and all extraneous parts consigned to the waves.

Williams was the last to finish his task. 'What a bloody waste,' he lamented as he dumped the expensive hardware over the side. 'I could have taken that home for my neighbour's kid to play with.'

'Fond of him, are you?' Donnelly asked innocently.

Williams shot him an evil grin. 'No, I hate the little bastard. With a bit of luck he'd have broken his bloody neck.'

'OK, cut the crap,' Graham barked. 'We've got to get moving.' He scrambled to his knees on the bucking hull of his windsurfer, grasping firmly the rope which would haul up the mast and sail. 'Now, everyone listen good. Once we cut apart and get moving, try to stay abreast of each other.

Make sure each one of you has everybody else in sight at all times. One of us gets lost out there, and there ain't gonna be any time to send out search parties. Anyone who *is* stupid enough to get isolated will head straight for the Turkish coast and beach where they can. You pay your own fare home.'

Willerbey, Donnelly and Williams all stared out over the black expanse of open sea and took the warning to heart. Even with the protection of a group, the journey ahead of them was formidable. Isolated and alone, it would be sheer hell.

Graham climbed to his feet, spreading them apart for balance and bracing himself with the rope against the wild, rolling motion of the waves. He gave the others a few seconds to follow suit and began to haul the sail out of the water.

It took Willerbey two attempts and Williams no fewer than four duckings before they were all upright, grasping the wishbones of their rigs firmly and holding the sails neutral to the wind.

'OK, let's go,' Graham yelled. Bracing himself, he dipped the forward edge of his sail into the wind and hauled back on the wishbone as it billowed out with a surge of power. As if suddenly yanked by a giant hand, the four craft seemed momentarily to jump out of the water, then climb to the top of the waves, skimming across them at ever-increasing speed.

30

Graham let go of the wishbone as the dark shape of the Russian ship came into view, allowing the mast and sail to fall into the water. He dropped to his belly on the flat hull, glancing sideways to check that his companions had followed his lead.

They had come up on the ship unexpectedly, approaching at a tangent which would have put them directly across its bows in less than a minute. The vessel was in virtual darkness, showing only a single light at the stern and a faint glow of illumination from the bridge. It was close, and its current course would bring it even closer before it started to move away from them again. Certainly too close for shouted conversation, Graham realized. He unwound the nylon cord from his waist, attached it to the mast as a safety line and rolled softly off the board into the water. With a slow, gentle breast-stroke, he began to swim over towards Willerbey's rig.

Willerbey waited until the man had draped one arm over his board and pulled himself up until their faces were only inches apart. The ship had now passed its closest point to them and was beginning to pull away. 'That's not a freighter,' he hissed quietly.

Graham shook his head. 'Frigate,' he whispered back. 'Riga class at a guess, and doing about eight knots – which would be about right for a night convoy in these waters. Looks like we've sailed right into the middle of the convoy, and they're shadowing our target a lot closer than we figured. The signal beacon suggests we're right on top of her.'

Donnelly and Williams had paddled their boards over to join them, just in time to overhear the last part of the whispered conversation.

'Shit, boss,' Donnelly hissed. 'How the hell are we going to get past half the Russian Navy?'

It was a good question, Graham thought. If his guess was correct, the waters immediately around them were busier than Cowes harbour in regatta week. And if the rest of the Russian fleet were in similar blackout operation to the frigate, getting through them was not going to be easy.

'Our best bet is probably going to be in out-flanking them,' he whispered after a moment's consideration. 'We skirt the rest of the convoy wide, home in on the freighter at an angle and then sail straight into her bow-wave. Then we pick our way along the side to the stern using the shadow under her hull for cover.'

Williams nodded reflectively. 'Sounds good to me,' he conceded. 'But can we outrun them in time? It's going to be first light in under two hours. Then we'll be sitting ducks. The bastards will be able to use us for target practice.'

'If this wind keeps up – no problem,' Graham murmured confidently. 'With a bit of luck we can close in with over an hour to spare.' He paused, adding the necessary proviso. 'But that's assuming we don't run into any unexpected problems, so keep your bloody eyes peeled.' He let go of Willerbey's board and dropped back into the water. 'Right, let's do it,' he hissed, beginning to swim back to his own rig.

Fired with a greater sense of urgency, all four men pulled up their sails on the first attempt and edged into the wind once again. Tacking off to starboard, Graham set a course which would take them directly across the wake of the Russian frigate. When they were clear of the main body of the Russian convoy, they could close in on the freighter on broad reach and at top speed.

Graham's estimates turned out to be a little optimistic. Their diagonal course proved to be slow going, and there were three more emergency stops as other Russian ships came into view at varying distances. At one stage, they found themselves sailing directly across the surface footprint of a submarine, which had obviously passed by at periscope depth only moments previously. By the time Graham considered it safe to set a direct course for the freighter, they had already used up the best part of an hour, and their target had opened up a gap of at least five miles. It was going to be tight, they all knew. Dangerously tight.

*　　*　　*

The first ominous signs of the impending dawn were already apparent as they finally closed in towards the side of the freighter. The overall blackness of the night was much lighter now, fading to a distinct shade of grey at the horizon point, where the sea and the sky could now be clearly identified as two separate entities.

Graham led them in fast, at an acute angle to the main bulk of the ship. Docking with the hull was going to be a tricky manoeuvre, requiring split-second timing and precision. The prow of his board cut into the bow-wave of the large vessel roughly amidships, and for a few horrible seconds it seemed as though he must slam right into her side. Then he dropped his sail, allowing the forward impetus of the windsurfer to be cancelled out by the repulsing effect of the ship's passage through the water. The board slowed and finally came to a stop only inches from the vessel's hull, slipping smoothly down its side towards the stern but already being pushed away again. His safety line attached, Graham slipped into the water and kicked out desperately against the effect of the bow-wave, reaching the ship's hull again and gingerly pressed his magnetic clamp into position against its metal plates.

As delicate as his movements had been, the sound seemed to echo over the water as though someone had struck a gong deep within the bowels of the ship. Graham felt his heart quicken, as a rush of adrenalin coursed through his system.

Fortunately the manoeuvre did not have to be

repeated by his companions. Instead they each in turn homed in on his floating board, now strung out from the side of the ship on the safety line, attached themselves and let their own rigs become buoys for the next man in line. Moments later the four windsurfers were trailing out across the bow-wave like the tail of a flying kite.

The three Marines joined Graham in the water, swimming in line towards him until Willerbey could clutch on to his leg and form the second link in a human chain. Finally all four men breathed an inner sigh of relief for small mercies, even though they were only temporarily secure and far from safe. The tricky part was over; now came the dangerous bit.

Holding grimly on to the magnetic clamp with one hand against the powerful tug of the bow-wave, Graham secured the safety line attached to his board to the device and grasped it again with both hands. Turning his head, he looked towards Donnelly, on the end of the line.

All the years of rigorous training, all the shared hardships and dangers, all the camaraderie of an exclusive and élite force were on the line now. One thing above all that an SBS man learned was that in a tight situation you had to be able to trust your fellow Marine with your life. That trust was now about to be tested to the full. The four of them were at their most vulnerable. One slip, one simple mistake or error of judgement and they would all be swept away from the side of the ship into the open sea, with little chance of survival or rescue.

Taking a deep breath, Graham nodded to Donnelly the signal that they were ready to make the next move. He held his breath deep in his lungs as the man turned his attention to Williams, setting up the next manoeuvre. Holding tightly to the man's arm, he turned in the water so that Williams safely passed along the last of Donnelly's clamps and he was able to change hands to relieve the tension.

Graham clipped the last of the devices to his belt and detached himself from Williams' ankle. Reaching up with the one in his free hand, he placed it as high as he could then hauled himself up out of the water, taking his full body weight on the strength of one arm. Slowly, agonizingly, hand over hand, he began to climb up the stern of the freighter.

31

Graham reached the top of the stern and pulled his head up slowly and cautiously over the rim, scanning the immediate deck area for any signs of life. Everything was quiet. Having pulled himself over the edge, Graham swung his feet soundlessly on to the deck and dropped into the shadows between one of the stern capstans and the side of the hull.

Quickly but stealthily, he unwound sufficient coils of the vessel's mooring rope and carried it back to the edge, then dropped it over the side for the rest of the men.

Light flared suddenly and briefly to the side of him. Graham whirled on the balls of his feet as a huge blond giant of a man stepped out of the gloom from where he had been sheltering against the wind, in the process of lighting a cigarette. The man gaped at Graham dumbly for a moment, still holding the extinguished match between his fingers as the freshly lit cigarette dropped from his lips to the deck.

Graham's mind raced. His first instinct was to rush the man immediately, but his training kept him in check. The distance between them was too great, giving the Russian plenty of time to prepare himself for any frontal attack. Perhaps more to the point, the sounds of a fight would be sure to alert other members of the crew, and besides, Blondie looked more than capable of taking care of himself. Graham froze, awaiting the next move. It was not long in coming.

The Russian deck-hand's initial surprise passed. His hand darted inside his shirt and came out clutching the butt of a 9mm Stechkin automatic pistol. So Pavlaski had been wrong about merchant seamen carrying weapons, Graham thought briefly. Or perhaps the Russians had known they were coming after all.

'Who are you? What are you doing?' the man barked in Russian, as he levelled the automatic at Graham's belly, his finger tightening around the trigger.

Graham thought fast, the years of high-intensity training in adapting and reacting to unfamiliar situations coming to his aid. His body stiffened in a more than passable imitation of a Russian military salute.

'Congratulations,' he said quietly and calmly, in the man's native language. 'You have intercepted me successfully. This will look good on your work record, comrade.'

Graham was close enough to see a momentary look of doubt and confusion flicker across the Russian's face. Obviously the man was not too bright, he realized with faint relief. He needed all the help he could get.

He allowed a thin smile to curl his lips, increasing the Russian's sense of bemusement. 'This is a military exercise to test the security of this vessel,' he went on in fluent Russian. 'You have done well. Now, please escort me to your captain so that I may pass on my commendation to him.'

This last master-stroke seemed to have done it, Graham thought, his hopes surging as the deck-hand's apelike face twitched and jumped with uncertainty. Graham could imagine little gears and cranks turning slowly inside the man's head.

The pistol in his hand quivered slightly, then dropped as sheer indecision made Blondie's decision for him. He was a simple merchant seaman, not at all accustomed to the unusual degree of naval activity which had accompanied this particular voyage. It was not for him to question the strange ways of the Russian military. He was dimly aware that he had accidentally done something right, and was being praised for it. Now he was to be commended to his captain, and there was the ghost of a hope in the back of his mind that some sort of reward might be in the offing. In the circumstances, it would appear foolish to do anything which might spoil things.

Holding the automatic at his side, he nodded curtly in Graham's direction, summoning him over. 'Come,' he said. 'I will take you to the captain.'

Graham smiled, moving towards the man. 'This is a fine ship you have here,' he said conversationally. 'Yes indeed, a fine ship.'

Blondie just grunted, half turning to lead the

way towards the bridge. It was the mistake which Graham had been waiting for. Leaping forward in a blur of movement, he closed the gap between them and brought the side of his hand down across the back of the Russian's neck in a vicious chop. Apart from releasing a sudden hiss of breath, the big man collapsed soundlessly, folding up on the deck like some outsized rag doll.

Graham dropped to his knees beside the man's crumpled form, every sense in his body in a state of full alert. If the conversation had been overheard by anyone, then they were in real trouble. His ears straining to catch the faintest sound, Graham was aware of Donnelly, Williams and Willerbey scrambling over the stern behind him, but other than that, the rest of the ship still remained as quiet as the proverbial grave. Taking the automatic pistol from Blondie's fingers, Graham tucked it into his belt. Martin's orders about no weapons were still very much in his mind, but circumstances had changed sufficiently for him to make a command decision. Now that crew members appeared to be armed after all, it seemed sensible to have a gun to at least brandish, if not actually use.

The other three Marines were all safely on deck now. Crouching low, they crept up to join Graham, peering down at the burly figure of the unconscious seaman.

'Jesus Christ, Sarge,' Willerbey whispered in his ear. 'What did it take to put him down? A fucking pile-driver?'

Graham flashed the man a nervous grin. 'We

just talked things over like two reasonable men,'
he hissed back.

He unzipped the front of his wetsuit, pulled
out a roll of sticky carpet tape and tore open
its waterproof plastic wrapping with his teeth.
After pinioning Blondie's arms behind his back,
he wrapped several layers of tape firmly around
his wrists and then secured his ankles. Then he
rolled the man on to his back and stuck a length
of tape over his mouth. Rising to his feet, he
stared out over the side of the freighter towards
the horizon, where a distinct glow heralded first
light. He pulled the other three Marines into a
tight huddle around him.

'Now listen, we're going to have to put our
bloody skates on,' he whispered. 'We don't have
time for any fucking subtleties. Circumstances call
for the direct approach.' Graham tapped the gun
in his belt, then jerked his finger in the direction
of the bridge before whispering in Willerbey's ear
again. 'You take Donnelly back to the stern and
skirt round the other side in case there are any
other crew on deck watch. Williams and I will
take care of the captain and the radio operator.
Give us exactly two minutes, and then join us on
the bridge.'

Willerbey nodded silently. With Donnelly close
behind him, he moved off stealthily in the direction
they had come from. Graham tapped Williams
briefly on the shoulder. 'Right, let's go,' he hissed,
tugging the Stechkin from his belt.

The Russian captain momentarily froze with

shock as the two Marines burst on to the bridge. His mouth, at first just gaping open, began to frame itself into a shout of alarm before a threatening wave of the automatic in Graham's hand changed his mind for him.

'One sound and I'll blow your head off,' Graham growled in Russian, reinforcing the gesture. He stepped back, still holding the gun pointed straight into the terrified man's face as Williams slapped tape over his mouth and bound his wrists behind his back. Graham pressed his lips close to the captain's ear. 'I have twenty heavily armed men crawling all over this ship,' he lied convincingly. 'One move from you in the next five minutes will get you and a large proportion of your crew killed. Do you understand that?'

The fear in the skipper's eyes showed that he believed the threat. He nodded his head emphatically.

'Good,' Graham hissed. He pushed the man down into a sitting position while Williams secured his legs. He waited until the Welshman had risen to his feet again before tossing him the gun. 'Go and take care of the radio,' he muttered. 'I'll keep watch from here.'

Williams nodded, moving off in the direction of the radio room. Moments later Graham heard a brief, muffled cry of surprise, followed by a dull thud, a faint groan and then silence. He imagined, rather than actually heard, the sounds of wires being ripped out of delicate equipment.

'Fix it?' he asked quietly as Williams rejoined him.

The man nodded, grinning. 'They won't be tuning in to Voice of America for a while, that's for sure,' he murmured.

Donnelly and Willerbey made their apperance, on cue to the second.

'See anyone?' Graham asked.

Willerbey shook his head. 'Not a soul. Maybe they figure that with all the floating hardware around them, they don't need to post a deck watch.'

Graham thought for a few seconds, then said: 'Let's find out for sure.' Taking the gun from Williams' hand, he bent over the Russian captain again and peeled back his gag gingerly. 'Besides the big fair-haired sailor, anyone else out there on deck?'

The captain shook his head, his eyes rolling wildly. He looked scared shitless, Graham thought, in little doubt that the man was telling the truth.

'Thanks,' he said politely, replacing the sticky tape over the man's mouth. 'Now don't you forget what I told you. Don't even try to move for at least five minutes, or all hell is going to break loose.'

Satisfied that the captain would do exactly as he was told, Graham looked at the other men. 'Right, let's get what we came for and get the hell out of here,' he said. 'God's going to turn the house lights on any minute now, and I don't want to be centre-stage when it happens.'

He turned to Willerbey. 'Got your map?'

'Sure.' Willerbey unzipped his wetsuit, pulled out a small, flat, waterproof envelope and tore it open. He pulled out the contents, unfolded the single sheet of paper and spread it out across the top of the bridge console. 'Let's just hope our friend Pavlaski has a good sense of direction.'

'And a good memory,' Donnelly put in. 'He hasn't been aboard a Russian ship for four years.'

Graham ignored the rather pessimistic aside. Everything depended now on the accuracy of Pavlaski's intelligence. There was little point in approaching the main cargo hatches, which would almost certainly be secured. Although they had brought enough plastic explosive to blow them if necessary, to do so in the present circumstances would be almost suicidal.

Graham studied the map, which was essentially a schematic layout of the interior of the ship, with a red marker-pen line superimposed over it to show them their best route. According to the Russian defector, it was possible to access the interior of the cargo hold from the ship's stores, via a small emergency bulkhead door which remained constantly unsecured for safety reasons, and could be opened manually.

That was the theory, at least. Now came the time to put it to the acid test. Graham memorized the route and tucked the map back inside his wetsuit. He took one quick, nervous glance out of the bridge window. It was possible to see clear to the prow of the freighter now, and parts of the deck were already beginning to show a dull glow as they reflected the ever-brightening horizon.

Graham turned back to his companions, forcing a cheerful grin. 'OK, let's move our arses.'

*   *   *

The emergency hatch was exactly where Pavlaski had said it would be. Willerbey stepped forward, grasping the wheel and wrenching it round. To his relief, it moved smoothly and effortlessly. Freeing the door, Willerbey swung it inwards into the main cargo hold.

It was black as pitch inside. Williams produced a small pen torch from inside his wetsuit and snapped it on, probing the interior of the hold with its thin beam as he stepped through the hatch and moved forward, clearing space for the rest of the men to follow him.

Huge crates were packed all around them, towering above their heads. Williams examined the nearest one carefully, reading the stencilled label clearly emblazoned on its side. He let out a scornful snort of derision. 'Agricultural machinery,' he muttered cynically. 'Who do the lying bastards think they're kidding?'

Turning on another torch, Graham pushed past him and led the way down a narrow passageway between the crates. 'Follow me,' he hissed over his shoulder. 'This is obviously the heavy goods area. Pavlaski said that the smaller units would probably be up ahead.'

The four Marines moved hurriedly down the passage, eventually entering a small, clear area where the large crates ceased and a new stack of smaller packing cases began. Graham swept his torch over the new area, letting out a grunt of satisfaction. 'This looks more like it,' he said quietly. 'Let's take a shufti at what we've got here.'

They had all come equipped with small, light-weight crowbars attached to their belts. The tools were needed now. Quickly and efficiently, each man moved to a separate position and began to prise open a sample of each different cargo stack.

Graham had opened a crate of 20mm shells. 'Nothing but bloody ammo here,' he whispered. 'Anyone found anything more interesting?'

Each man gave a negative answer. Graham cursed, then flashed his torch over his watch. 'Christ, we're running out of bloody time,' he hissed in frustration. 'The fucking stuff's got to be around here somewhere.'

Donnelly had moved to a stack of about a dozen tall, upright packing cases, each about the size of a large filing cabinet. The dimensions didn't look promising, but they were running out of other crates to open. None too optimistically, he began to prise one of the side slats loose. Inside there were a dozen smaller crates, stacked on top of one another.

Turning towards Graham, he called out softly: 'Hey, Sarge. Come over here. This looks more like it.' He continued to dismantle the outer crate as Graham crept over to join him.

Graham snatched one of the smaller packages as soon as he could pull it free. It was the size of a small suitcase, and remarkably light for its apparent bulk. He felt a surge of hope as he set it down gently on the floor and started to open it. Although it was considerably larger than the briefcase size Martin had suggested, its general shape was right and anyway they had more or less exhausted all other possibilities.

The top of the packing case came off cleanly in one piece. Graham bent over it and examined the contents closely under the full beam of the torch. A surge of elation rippled through him as he realized they had found what they were looking for.

'Bingo,' he breathed, his relief showing clearly on his face. 'We just struck gold.'

He dived into his wetsuit and pulled out the large waterproof plastic sack each man had brought specifically for transporting the units back to base. Carefully pulling the double lines of ridged hermetic seals apart, he slid it over the guidance system module and pressed the seals shut again. The sack came equipped with webbing and shoulder straps. With Donnelly's help, he slipped the unit into position across his back like a bergen and rose to his feet, testing the weight of his load. It was bearable, although it would slow him down considerably, and carrying it back down the stern of the ship would be far from easy. Once they got back to their rigs he would have to lash the unit to the hull of the sailboard. Trying to operate a windsurfer with that load on his back would be impossible.

He hissed over to Williams and Willerbey. 'OK, let's get the hell out of here.' He turned to move. Donnelly clutched at his arm.

'The boss said get two,' he pointed out.

Graham shook his head. 'They're bigger and

heavier than we figured. And we just ran out of time. The boffins will have to make do with one.'

Donnelly did not feel like arguing. Mutely, he followed Graham back down the passage between the crates as Williams and Willerbey fell in behind him.

Graham breathed a sigh of relief as they crept out on deck again. It was still not as light as he had feared it would be, although dawn must now be perilously close. They had perhaps ten minutes to get clear of the Russian convoy before they were open targets, he estimated. It would give them a start, and a fighting chance – but not much more than that. He led the way up the side of the ship and past the bridge, retracing their earlier footsteps towards the stern.

The big deck-hand had recovered consciousness, and although still groggy, was starting to struggle with his sticky bonds. Graham stopped by his side, quickly bending down to examine the man's wrists. The tape had started to stretch and give slightly. Given the man's obvious strength, he should be able to get his hands free well within the five minutes Martin had specified. He would of course then go directly to the bridge and free the captain. Shortly after that the shit would hit the fan.

32

Graham had seriously underestimated Blondie's brute strength. They were less than two hundred yards clear of the freighter's hull before a red distress flare curved into the sky behind them and exploded. Turning his head, Graham was just in time to see the chattering light of an Aldis lamp start to flash out its emergency message across the sea from the ship's bridge.

'Oh shit,' he roared at the top of his voice. There was no need for silence at that particular moment, and the chance to express his frustration so forcibly afforded him a certain sense of satisfaction, if not relief.

'Looks like they're on to us, Sarge,' Willerbey called out, rather superfluously. 'What say we split and run? Individually we'll be smaller targets and less easy to spot. They'll have to come after us singly, which is going to burn up time. Might give you a chance to get away with the swag.'

'Negative,' Graham yelled back. 'We stay together for the time being – or at least until we're actually spotted. Then we might have to think again.'

Willerbey was unconvinced. 'Jesus, you don't

actually think we can outrun the bastards, do you?'

Graham didn't – not for a minute – but for the sake of the men he summoned up an air of false bravado. 'We can fucking well try,' he shot back. 'These are bloody Russians, don't forget. They're not exactly too hot on individual action and personal initiative. It's going to take them a good ten minutes to figure out precisely what's happened, and get someone to take a decision about what action to take. If we're out of visual range by then, there's no way they can track us on their instruments, so they're going to have to rely on a sweep-search pattern. And there's a whole lot of fucking sea out there.'

'You sound bloody convincing, Sarge,' Donnelly yelled across the water. 'Now tell us about Father Christmas.'

'Up yours,' Graham barked back. 'Now let's cut the bloody cackle and make like flying fish.'

Having hauled in the sails tightly against the wind to convert the last erg of its power into forward speed, the four windsurfers skimmed across the crest of the choppy swell towards the glowing horizon.

The fast-attack craft seemed to materialize out of the blinding glare of the dawn sun like a ghost ship, homing in towards them at full speed.

Graham's heart sank. Even from a distance, the sleek lines of the vessel suggested that it would have a top speed in excess of thirty knots, making it totally impossible to outrun. Just when he was beginning to think that they had evaded the main bulk of the Russian convoy, he reflected bitterly. Just when he was beginning to dare hope that they had a chance. The approaching ship must have been out on a particularly wide flank, well away from the main body of the escort.

'Well, what now?' Donnelly yelled. 'Looks like we're really fucked this time.'

It was a pretty realistic assessment, Graham thought, and it would have been openly stupid to argue with it.

'Yeah, maybe,' he conceded. 'But we can still make it difficult for the bastards, give them a run for their money. Wait until she's right on top of us and then split out either side of her bows. That'll confuse them for a few seconds, and at the speed she's running, it'll take her another minute or so to turn around. Then they'll have to decide which of us to chase first.'

Even as he spoke, Graham knew he was offering the men no real hope, for there was none. At best, his strategy would only postpone the inevitable. Eventually, when the Russian skipper tired of the game of cat and mouse, he would probably put powered inflatables over the side to hunt them down individually, he guessed. Then it would all be over. With this fact in mind, he wondered for a moment whether it was worth bothering at all.

He dismissed the thought from his mind. Of course it was worth bothering. No one could ever say that the men of the SBS went down without a bloody good fight.

The approaching boat was almost upon them

now, and appeared to be slowing. Perhaps its skipper had anticipated his plan, Graham thought, then rejected the idea. Far more likely that he had just assumed that they would give up meekly, knowing they were cornered. He tensed himself for the optimum moment to order the dispersion.

He was about to call out to the men when a message in perfect English boomed out over the water from a megaphone aboard the ship. 'Sergeant Graham. Please tell your men to heave to and await pick-up. This is not a Russian vessel. We are here to help you.'

Graham's initial surge of elation was tempered with caution. Martin had made it quite clear that no pick-up attempt would be made until they were within Cypriot territorial waters – and he estimated that they were still many miles outside that protection. Could it possibly be a trick? It seemed highly unlikely. He had been greeted by name, and there was no way that could have become known to the Russians so quickly, if at all. On the face of it, it would appear that they were about to be rescued, although it seemed almost unbelievable that their pick-up vessel would have ventured so close to the pursuing Russian patrol. It was taking an incredible risk, and one that increased by the second if he wasted time thinking when he should be acting. It was this last realization that tipped the balance. Graham dropped his sail into the water and called out to the men.

'You heard what the man said, fellers. Looks like the Fifth Cavalry's here.'

With whoops of relief and gratitude, Willerbey, Donnelly and Williams followed his lead, sitting down on their boards as the rescue vessel cruised in towards them and someone dropped a rope ladder over the side.

'Please make this as fast as possible,' the voice over the megaphone urged. 'You've all been very naughty boys and you have some very angry Russians on your tail.'

Graham appreciated the humour, while accepting the very real urgency of the situation. He busied himself unlashing his precious package from the hull as the ship pulled alongside.

There was something wrong. Graham felt a distinct sense of unease as he clambered aboard the deck of the rescue vessel. He stared at the sallow, unsmiling face of the young sailor who had helped him up over the top of the rope ladder. The man was obviously not British, and somehow he didn't look like a Cypriot, either. What was even more disconcerting was the Uzi sub-machine-gun which dangled from his shoulder.

'Who the hell are you? What's going on here?' Graham demanded, suddenly very suspicious.

The sailor frowned. 'Please, we don't have time to talk now. Just let's get the rest of your men aboard and get out of here. Everything will be explained, I promise you.'

He didn't have a great deal of choice, Graham realized. He stood mutely aside as Williams reached the top of the ladder and scrambled aboard.

Willerbey and Donnelly were still in the water, frantically paddling their boards towards the side of the ship. Another member of the crew produced a coil of rope and threw them a tow-line, which Willerbey grabbed gratefully.

'You don't look too happy, Sarge,' Williams observed, noting the worried expression on Graham's face.

'I'm bloody well not. I think we're in some sort of trouble here, and I don't know what it is.'

Williams took a closer look at the crew members, and got the general picture. He fell silent as Willerbey and Donnelly were hauled aboard and the ship's four powerful diesel engines fired up to full power. After executing a tight circle in the water, the vessel headed off in the direction it had come from, quickly building up to full speed again.

'Please, follow me,' the young sailor said politely, showing the SBS men towards the interior of the vessel. 'As I said, everything will be explained.'

They were shown into a comfortable but sparsely furnished cabin. The sailor stood guard on the inside of the door, cradling his Uzi in an efficient but unthreatening grip. An adjoining door opened suddenly, and Selina Tsigarides stepped in to join them. She was dressed in a camouflage combat uniform, and was also toting an Uzi.

The Marines gaped at her in total incomprehension. Selina merely smiled. 'Please relax, all of you,' she urged. 'You are aboard a vessel of the Israeli Navy and you are all perfectly safe.'

Graham found his voice at last. 'Relax?' he said

gruffly. 'We've got half the bloody Russian fleet after us, we're aboard a ship we're not supposed to be aboard – and you tell us to relax.'

Selina nodded. 'Yes, Sergeant Graham. That's exactly what I want you to do. This is a Saar-class fast-attack craft, easily capable of a 1000-mile sustained run at a top speed of thirty knots. There is absolutely nothing in that Russian convoy which can touch us. We'll be docking in Haifa before you know it – where, incidentally, you will all be reunited with one of your colleagues, John Crewes.'

'John's alive?' Willerbey blurted out.

'Alive and perfectly unharmed,' Selina assured him. 'In fact, we've been treating him like a king, partly to make up for having to kidnap him in the first place. It wasn't something we actually planned, you understand, but his nocturnal training session gave us rather a good opportunity to place one of our own homing beacons inside the tubing of his rig, and we had to seize it. Obviously, we couldn't let him go afterwards, so we took him with us.'

Graham's head was spinning as he tried to make sense of it all. 'You bugged our rigs?' he asked incredulously.

Selina nodded calmly. 'Of course. How do you think we were able to find you so easily?'

'Then this whole caper was planned from the start?' Graham said. 'Any chance of you telling us why?'

The girl shrugged. 'I see no reason why not. We have every intention of being completely open with your government, and cooperating in every way possible.' Selina paused for a moment. 'As you may have already worked out for yourselves, I am an undercover agent for the Israeli Secret Service. When a whisper about Operation Windswept first came to us via one of our London operatives, we knew that we had to put our own cover operation into place.'

'Why?' Willerbey asked, still not understanding.

'I should have thought that was quite obvious,' Selina shot back. 'It is our country which is in the direct firing line of those missiles, after all. We weren't at all sure that we could fully trust the British government to share their knowledge of this new guidance system with us, so we decided to get hold of it ourselves. British scientists and military personnel will of course be perfectly welcome to come and join in every stage of the dismantling and decoding operation. We are more than willing to pool all our knowledge.'

At last it all began to make sense. 'So we've been bloody hijacked?' Graham said darkly, feeling a vague sense of outrage.

Selina flashed him a sardonic smile. 'Rather strong language, Sergeant, coming from someone who has just carried out an act of piracy on the high seas.'

She did have a point, Graham conceded. He fell silent, allowing the girl to continue.

'So, using my cover as a liaison officer for the Greek military, I penetrated your operation and kept tabs on the mission while we formulated our own backup plans,' she explained. 'The rest you know, and everything seems to have worked out rather well. Both our governments get exactly what they want, and the Russians will be too embarrassed to do a thing about it.'

Graham was silent for a long time after Selina finished. Despite a smouldering resentment at having been outsmarted at his own game, he couldn't help feeling a grudging sense of admiration for the way it had been accomplished. And the Israelis had pulled their arses out of the fire, after all.

'There's just one thing I don't quite understand,' he said. 'Your people are not exactly amateurs at this sort of thing. If you knew about the Russian shipment as well, why didn't you simply plan your own hijacking operation?'

Selina smiled warmly. 'You're quite right, Sergeant. As you say, our people are not amateurs, but they are realists. We are also honest enough to admit that there are experts in every field, and there are also master craftsmen. In short, if any group of men in the world were capable of pulling this operation off, it was the SBS. So of course we left it to you.'

The compliment went a long way towards restoring Graham's sense of proportion. He was unable to keep a warm smile of pride from creeping over his face. 'I'll drink to that,' he said.

Selina nodded. 'Indeed you shall. In fact we brought several bottles of champagne and brandy along expressly for that purpose. It's a long way to Haifa, gentlemen. I think if you start now, you have a more than reasonable chance of getting quite religiously pissed before we get there.'

OTHER TITLES IN SERIES FROM 22 BOOKS

Available now at newsagents and booksellers or use the order form provided

continued overleaf . . .

All at £4.99 net

All 22 Books are available at your bookshop, or can be ordered from:

22 Books
Mail Order Department
Little, Brown and Company
Brettenham House
Lancaster Place
London WC2E 7EN

Alternatively, you may fax your order to the above address.
Fax number: 0171 911 8100.

Payments can be made by cheque or postal order, payable to
Little, Brown and Company (UK), or by credit card (Visa/
Access). Do not send cash or currency. UK, BFPO and Eire
customers, please allow 75p per item for postage and packing,
to a maximum of £7.50. Overseas customers, please allow £1
per item.

While every effort is made to keep prices low, it is sometimes
necessary to increase cover prices at short notice. 22 Books
reserves the right to show new retail prices on covers which
may differ from those previously advertised in the books or
elsewhere.

NAME ....

ADDRESS ....

....

....

☐ I enclose my remittance for £_____
☐ I wish to pay by Access/Visa

Card number

☐☐☐☐ ☐☐☐☐ ☐☐☐☐ ☐☐☐☐

Card expiry date

☐☐ ☐☐

Please allow 28 days for delivery. Please tick box if you do not
wish to receive any additional information ☐